# Cobalt City
# Timeslip

Edited by
C. Dombrowski

Direct all orders to:
Timid Pirate Publishing
509 N. 85th St. #14,
Seattle, WA 98103

www.timidpirate.com

Printed in the United States of America
First Printing: October, 2010
ISBN: 978-0-615-40218-5

Other adventures in the Cobalt City Universe:

*Chanson Noir*

*Cobalt City Blues*

*Greetings from Buena Rosa*

*Ride Like the Devil*

*Cobalt City Christmas*

Revised Editions forthcoming in 2011.

# TIMESLIP

## Editor's Note

Welcome to tales of heroes, villains and the extraordinary.

This anthology combines stories from across time and space, centered on the imaginary metropolis of Cobalt City, where masked heroes and villains save and threaten the populace. From individual heroes making their names to the famed, merchandised team known as the Protectorate, the citizens have many names to call when danger threatens in the night.

These stories stand alone, but are enriched by the history and texture of a shared universe created by friends and authors over a period of many years. If this is your introduction to Cobalt City, enjoy the glimpse into the history and future of a remarkable place. To returning voyagers, welcome back!

Tantalized? Craving more? A wide variety of Cobalt City novels are available—with revised editions coming in 2010-2012 from Timid Pirate Publishing. From inception in Nathan Crowder's novels to ongoing anthologies, the tales continue to grow and thrive.

Happy exploring.

*C. Dombrowski, Editor*

# TIMESLIP

## Cobalt City Overview

Where is Cobalt City? If you want to be in movies, you go to Hollywood. You want to make it big in country music, you go to Nashville. But if you want to make it big in the cape and cowl game, you go to Cobalt City.

In the imagined universe of these stories, Cobalt City was the site of some of the stranger battles of the American Revolutionary War, where French General Lafayette played a major part. Located just south of Boston on the Massachusetts coast, the City has the first recorded instance of a masked hero in the United States.

Since then, the heroes have flocked to the city. Those that die are buried in the large park bearing Lafayette's name. The once-military emplacement of the Cannonade along the coast by the 20th century has been turned into a hipster neighborhood full of old brick and concrete buildings climbing with ivy and narrow streets. The luxury high-rise condos, boutiques, and galleries along the park's long east and west sides provide a buffer between the University of Cobalt City on the north end and the decrepit Hollows on the south end.

The hills to the west feature the neighborhood of Karlsburg, where immigrant communities of many cultures transposed bits and pieces of their homeland into a diverse mosaic. The sleepy bedroom community of Morriston borders to the north with suburbs, malls, and planned housing. Across the river to the south, Regency Heights' palatial estates on a wooded bluff are mere minutes from Quayside's glitzy casinos. In Quayside, gambling was legalized in the 1940s. The working class Quayside neighborhood scrapes by amid the factories, docks, and warehouses, spreading all the way west to Buzzard's Bay.

Do you need to know more about Cobalt City to enjoy the anthologies? No. Could it make the experience richer? Yes. For example, take stories from this collection, like "Vengeance on the Layover" by de Bie or

# TIMESLIP

"Daddy's Little Girl" by Vogel. Both stories use different incarnations of The Huntsman as well as characters created by the authors. While it's cool to know that his legacy stretches back to the Revolutionary War, that isn't necessary. Kemp's story plays with the history of Cobalt City, but "I Blame Management," is Jax's first published adventure. Zimmerman's Devil Cat and Imp return in "Girl's Night Out," but though the story picks up in the middle of the action, that action is unrelated to previous stories. Wrecker of Engines is the great uncle of the Protectorate's Wild Kat, but that doesn't prepare you for Jones' "Claws of the Dragon Queen."

And "The War at Home" gave me the chance to play with the concept of avatars explored in *Chanson Noir*, *Cobalt City Blues*, and *Ride like the Devil*. Despite that and the appearance of a special guest star, everything you need to know is between these covers.

*Nathan Crowder, Fall, 2010*

# TIMESLIP

## Table of Contents

# TIMESLIP

## A Newer Shade of Blue
### Pre-Columbian era

Every year the spring star fire rains down on the people and the planting begins. Every year the autumn star fire falls on the people and the harvest begins. When the coils of the silver river spoke are at their brightest, those of the people who dare the frost and cold, those who must hunt in the winter and those who count the moons know the longest night is over and the light will return.

Except the season it didn't.

That was the season when the sun refused her vows to her husband the earth. With only his cold white blanket and his cold second wife the moon, he refused to let anything grow. The days grew longer and longer but the sun was nowhere to be seen. Even in the clear blue sky before the spring star fire she would not come thaw the cold heart of her husband.

Then the star fire fell, never before or since had it fallen so heavily. Then the wailing began, the sound of heartbreak and injury. The sun had gotten caught in the star fire, she appeared brighter and brighter, falling faster and faster. She fell weeping and screaming into the arms of her husband the earth; tearing him from the sea to the mountains in her grief and injury.

He began weeping, clear tears of the earth, for having ever believed she would abandon him. From then to now his tears filled her fateful trench.

The people were afraid, except for one boy. He knew that sound of crying, it was the same sound of crying that his mother made when she hurt her leg and couldn't walk. So he went to help the sun.

As he got closer to her he felt strong. As he got closer he moved faster, so fast he didn't even touch the ground any more; so strong he thought he could lift anything, even the sun.

When he got to the sun, she was so hot he could barely touch her and was so bright he could barely see. In her crackling voice of flame and light, she told him to bring his friends and she would give

I

them the same gifts if they would help her back into the sky. He flew back and soon his friends were running into flight as well.

She promised that if they lifted her back into the sky, she would give these gifts to many people who live by the river by the sea. So they lifted her up & up & up. They were never seen again, but the sun was. She whispered her promise to the people and she kept it. Many who were strong and fast came to the place where the river meets the sea. Many who were wild and clever, too.

When the pale men built their blue city on the river by the sea the heroes still came, as did the villains.

The sun keeps her promises...

### For Edwardo Galliano

*Michaela Hutfles. Ms. Hutfles lives in the Pacific Northwest. A Project Manager by day and a locovore by night this is her first published story. Inspired by Cobalt City's denizens and Eduardo Galiano's "Memory of Fire" trilogy she thought, "what the hell, let's put them together." This is the result of such thinking.*

# TIMESLIP

## Vengeance on the Layover
### 2005

No fucking robots.

That's one of my rules—always has been, always will be.

If it's got circuits instead of brains, gears instead of muscles, or antennae instead of goody bits, I stay as far away as possible, thanks very much.

But standing here at Cobalt International Airport, staring up at the robotic departures sign and focusing all my force of will at the ticker next to my connecting flight, I realize just how close I am to breaking my rule. If that's what it would take—to get the glorified scrabble letters on the big board to spell out "arrived" or "on-time" or "ludicrously late, but still coming," rather than "delayed" or—now—"cancelled," I would do it.

I'd break my rule.

I'd fuck a robot.

But really, the closest I'd get would be some no-brain switchboard operator guy, and he wouldn't be able to do anything about it. You can't just conjure lost or grounded 737s out of thin air.

Well, unless, that is, you're one of the technosavants I know (and may or may not have slept with), but that's a different story.

I wonder if one of them has a superplane for rent and would lend it to me on credit.

Vivienne Cain's Great Tuscan Vacation™ was all Andre's idea. (Note to self: fire Andre when you get back.) "It'll be just like that movie," he said. "Wandering the Italian countryside, finding romance and excitement . . . you know the one . . ."

"High Plains Drifter?" I suggested.

"Tsch!" Andre was getting into the fantasy now, the way he sometimes did. One little smartass crack like that would barely faze him. "You know, the wine, the dancing, *ciao bella!*"

He blew a kiss to everyone in the room, which consisted of two permanent fixtures attached to their barstools to watch Adult Swim.

# TIMESLIP

They returned a drunken look of long tolerance.

"And you'll meet a beautiful man there with eyes like the sea after a storm, and a smile that makes your knees shake—"

"Clint Eastwood?" I said. "Pre-crazy Mel Gibson?"

The one-two punch got him, and he gave me a petulant frown. "Honey," he said. "Now you're just showing your *age*."

So thanks to Andre, here I am: single white female on the wrong side of forty traveling by herself on a day-long plane trip to the sunniest and apparently happiest place on earth for a woman past her prime.

Lucky me.

Luckier still that my layover in Cobalt City seems to have gone past "temporarily delayed due to lightning storms with no apparent cause" (typical for a weekend, really) to "indefinitely delayed due to meteorological catastrophe of unknown cause." Yay.

The desk attendant, at least, is helpful if entirely too perky. With her blue uniform, sensible pumps, and flair, she could be a career waitress if not for the Unified Airlines nametag. "It's just one or another of them, you know," she says brightly.

"Sure," I say, my tone exposing every ounce of fascination I can muster.

There are other travelers streaming around us, heading toward baggage claim or connection flights. A good-looking kid pauses and looks at me funny—like he recognizes me. I look away, back to the desk lady.

"It's just how Cobalt City gets," she says, as though I didn't understand. "Especially around Valentine's Day."

"Right."

"You know super-villains," she says. "They're all terribly misunderstood, and they get something out of blowing up all those buildings and making people scared and—"

"Listen," I say. "I've been flying for eighteen hours today—can we make this snappy? "

"Oh, you poor dear!" she exclaims. She looks at me

sympathetically. "Had some trouble with the Expedia, did we?"

"Something like that."

I blame it on Andre. The aforementioned eighteen hours comprised four stops to get me to the east coast, with layovers in cities he'd never heard of but were "probably" close together.

She taps her keys. "I can book you on the next flight to Venice at . . . nine."

I check the watch on the inside of my wrist. "I don't suppose you mean *nine*, like two hours ago?"

"Sorry, I meant nine a.m. tomorrow."

"Of course you did."

"That or the eleven." She taps more, checks her screen, and furrows her brow. "Oh no! It looks like all the airport hotels are booked up!"

"Of course they are."

The temptation rises in me to do something about the overwhelming enthusiasm to help me, but I chalk that impulse up to the tiredness and the lack of liquor.

"Do you want that flight?"

"Yeah." I look up, and see the silver lining in all this. "Better make it the eleven."

"Tired after all that flying, I guess," she says.

"Nope, I plan to be very hung over. This airport has a bar, right?"

She points. "Well, there is this one bar . . ."

"Sounds perfect!" I step away from the desk and head to the airport bar, which has one thing Italy doesn't: two of my best friends—Jim and Jack—and a night-long supply.

In retrospect, waking up six hours later—with a splitting headache and dressed like *this*—maybe the bar was a bad idea.

I notice the kid staring at me around drink four or five. I lose count sometimes.

(OK, every time.)

Anyway, in the mirror behind the bar, I notice the kid watching me from the entrance. Handsome and tanned, he's the sort of guy who could wear a muscle shirt without looking like a tool but chooses not to. That blue sweatshirt does well enough. I realize, however, he can't be more than seventeen, and since that means he could be *my* kid (if I'd made some dodgy decisions earlier in life), I don't look any harder.

The bartender pours another double on the rocks, which is exactly what I need.

The stool squeaks next to me at the bar. A man sits down—fortyish, business suit, management hair brushed with silver at the temples. "Hey," he says.

That's it? No cheesy line or anything?

"Hey," I say.

He gestures at my drink. "I see that's Jim Beam you're drinking."

"Yup," I say, turning my glass so the ice clinks. "Did you have an alternate suggestion, Whiskey Man?"

"Confident dame like you?"

I arch one black eyebrow. "Dame?"

He pulls a flask wrapped in blue silk from his coat. "I'd say Johnnie Walker Blue."

"Seriously?" I eye the flask. "And you keep it in a flask?"

"Sure." He has three little creases on his cheek—an old scar that looks somehow familiar.

"Sorry, I don't take drinks from strange men."

"OK then." He pulls a black leather wallet from inside his coat and gives me—of all things—a business card.

"Erich Manh Coelm," I read. "That's a mouthful."

"Never had any complaints."

The bartender brings us two glasses, and Coelm pours us two drinks. Sure enough, it's blue label—I can tell by how it looks, how it smells . . . I make sure to let him drink some of his before I touch mine. Now *that* is good scotch.

"Coelm," I say. "German? Or Jewish?"

"Both," he says. "My great uncle was Albert Einstein."

"No shit."

"None."

I finish my glass, and he refills it. Awesome.

"OK, Einstein," I say. "Of all the words you could have picked, why 'confident'?"

He shrugs. "Well, you *know* you're 'good-looking,' and 'smart' sounds lame."

"*Wicked* lame." I see the light, callused line around the third finger on his left hand—the shadow of an absent ring—which tells me enough. Not that it scares me—I am *confident*, after all. "Does your wife know you like to use creative lines on liquored up women in bars?"

He shrugs. "Only when they're her."

I like him. He's an asshole, but he's my kind of asshole. Good-looking, rich, and he carries around Johnnie Walker Blue in a flask. What's not to love?

He pulls a hundred out of his black leather wallet. "How much?"

Ah yes. That.

Now, I know what I should do in this instance. A woman in my profession, with the sort of getups it's landed me in, has occasionally run into misunderstandings like this. But the whiskey in his flask was strong, so instead I flirt a little. "You wanna buy me a bottle of something, big spender? Blue label's at least two hundred."

He considers me a moment, then pulls out another hundred.

This time, I laugh. "Add another fifty and we've got a Dom Perignon."

He frowns. "You must be really high-class—five hundred? A thousand?"

Men, in my experience, do not like to be laughed at, particularly where their money is concerned. But it's so god-damned funny that I can't resist a giggle. (Also, if I'd learned I could get that much, I'd have started turning tricks years ago when I had no shame—given up on this whole capes business and all the fat lot of nothing good it's brought me.)

I think about it now. Ordinarily, I'd tell this asshole off, but I'm just drunk enough to consider how much more comfortable a stranger's bed is compared to a set of three airport seats and no pillow. Plus, he's cute in a sleazy sort of way.

Ultimately, my laughter makes my decision for me.

His face starts turning red, but that only makes it funnier. I burst out loud enough to draw the attention of everyone in the bar. "Listen, Ernie or whatever your name is, go back to your wife, all right? Buy her some flowers. Possibly chocolate."

He looks startled. His hands clench and relax several times, as though with a mind of their own. Then he sneered. "Come on, you *know* you want it. I'm exactly your type— *exactly.*"

"Exactly *wrong,*" I say. "Look, I'm not sure where we got off on the wrong foot, but unless they've update the O.E.D. since last I checked, 'no' still means 'get the fuck away from me,' so make with the getting the fuck—"

Then he puts his hand on my arm. Big mistake.

Normally, I don't use my powers in public—it's kind of a thing. But after six glasses of whiskey and some asshole in a suit getting hands-y, they sort of do their own thing.

Darkness coils around us, feeding on fear, drawing it into me and changing me. This is how my power manifests—the better the fear, the more effective.

And this one? It's a doozy.

"Strong women scare you, do they?"

My eyes turn jet black, and my skin grows paler than usual. My clothes swirl and shift into deep purple robes. I become greater, but not physically. There is no need for ostentation. I grasp his arm with fingers so strong they could crush cars like aluminum cans.

His eyes widen, and I lean in close. "I asked nicely once. That's all you get."

Then I throw him back, and he topples out of his chair onto the floor. From there, he stares up at me with a look both fearful and a little admiring. Then he scoops up whatever dignity he has left and buggers off. The glamour fades as he goes away, and I see that he's left his flask with its precious contents.

I try to use my dark powers for good, you know.

I realize, after I've downed two more shots from the asshole's flask, that I'm not alone. "Can I help you?" I ask in a tone that clearly indicates he'd better say no.

The kid—it's the kid from before—straightens. He looks excited. He's holding something vaguely notebook-shaped in his hands. "You *are* her, aren't you?"

There are many ways one might answer this sort of question, my favorite at the moment being the swift application of deadly force. But as blowing up whole terminals without at least proper introductions between combatants is considered in bad taste, I decide to play this one cool. At least, as cool as the liquor allows. "Huh?" I say.

Smooth, V—very smooth.

"You know who I mean." He puts what he was holding on the table—it's a comic book.

Great.

One dexterous brown finger indicates the woman on the cover: dark hair, pale skin, one leg dangling from where she sits on a bar, a bottle of Tennessee whiskey close to hand. She's dressed all in black, down to lipstick and nails. The only sparkle of color comes from the blood-stained silver claw—a nasty thing half-brass knuckles, half-medieval gauntlet—that hangs from her right hand like a casually-held gun.

The kid taps the title of the book. "*Lady Vengeance*," he reads. "That's you, isn't it?"

"Nope," I say. "Not even a little bit."

He doesn't look convinced. "I knew it was you when you used your power on that suit. What was he? A spy? Super-villain?"

"*That* was some jerk who thought I was . . . something I'm not," I say. "Speaking of which, I'm not a MILF, not a cougar, and certainly not a spring fling. So what are you doing talking to me?"

His expression immediately gets nervous. "Well, I just—I don't know . . ."

Shit. Here I was hoping for a super-villain or an assassin or something, and I got something worse: a fan.

"OK, fine," I say. "I'm her, all right? Happy?"

He extends his hand. "Marcus Castile," he says. "The Huntsman."

I look blearily at his hand. "Huntsman?"

He looks decidedly uncomfortable. "In, um, the Icons, and—"

"Oh sure, the guy with the bow and armor—I know him," I say. "I just thought the Huntsman was more my age than yours."

"Oh, you're thinking of my father, Vincent."

"Thanks," I say.

"Huh?"

"Nothing." Age is one of those things that just happens. "So you're a cape?"

"Yep!" His face brightens. "You inspired me, you know. I mean, it's the family business, but if I hadn't had the comics about Supergroup, I might have become, I don't know, like a physical trainer or something." He smiles even wider. "Ooh, and I loved your spin-off, too."

"Thanks, I guess," I said. "They always made my boobs bigger in those things."

"Oh, I don't know, I think—ahem." He looks back up at my eyes. "Listen, are you . . . are you in town for a while? I bet the rest of the Protectorate would love to meet you. We just got back from our first mission. That's who you turned into, by the way—the Queen of the Black Sigh. I guess you got my fear—"

"That sounds great and all—really," I say. "But I've got a flight in the morning."

"Oh, OK," he says, sounding a little disappointed. "In case you change your mind, I'll give you our number. We're unlisted—secret lair and stuff."

"Yeah, sure."

I look around for something to write on, and settle on that Coelm guy's business card. Marcus writes the digits on the back.

"Did you want an autograph or something?" I ask. "I don't do pictures, so don't ask."

"No, that's . . . that's OK." He frowns, considering. I can tell I'm upsetting him, which is not all that unusual. I have that effect. "I did have one question, though," he says.

"Shoot."

"You and Antonio Desantes—you know, the Raven?"

"No," I say. "I mean, yes, I know him, but—no, we didn't have a thing."

He got that shrewd look in his eye that only canon wonks can muster. "But in issue 15 of Lady Vengeance, it seemed like you did. Pretty clearly."

I glare at him.

"OK, OK, I get it," he says. He points at my purse. "Give me a call sometime—I mean, the Protectorate."

"Sure," I say. Like that's gonna happen.

He goes away, casting back one glance followed by a sigh and shake of his head.

So he wasn't happy to meet me—one of his idols, apparently. *Hey kid, join the club.*

I have another shot of Johnnie Walker, and things get a little fuzzy.

When next I wake up, it feels like an angry badger is trying to burrow out of my head through the longest path available—down my throat to my stomach. My vision sways up and down, like the world's on an elevator and I'm just watching. Being drunk *and* hung over sucks.

A light buzzes overhead, reflecting off sterile gray walls. I grope in the bright light and my fingers click metallically around a silvery guidebar. My other hand covers my aching eyes. I'm sitting on cold porcelain: a toilet. I'm in the disabled stall in a public restroom.

"Well, *someone's* a kinky boy," I murmur, my voice slurred.

Then my eyes focus on the hand in front of my face—a hand wrapped in black leather.

"Fuck," I say.

I look at my other hand next, the one clinging to the guidebar. I'm wearing a clawed glove, the barbs digging into the plaster wall.

Oh no.

I look down at my body. Sure enough, I'm wearing the outfit I saw on that Marcus kid's comic book: my old-school, black leather, hilariously slutty Lady Vengeance costume.

"OK, now *that's* fucked up," I say.

Outside the stall, I hear the water switch on, and my whole body tenses. Fuck. I don't know where I am, what's going on, or what's waiting out there. I reach out with my power, but I get a whole lot of hazy nothing. Maybe it's the scotch—how much of it did I drink? Was there something in it?

Slowly, flexing my talon, I push the unlocked door open. At the sink stands a shirtless, well-muscled man with dark hair plastered to his scalp and neck. At first, I catch my breath, sure it's the kid, but no. The three little scars on his cheek are livid red. It's the asshole from the bar.

No, it isn't. I know this guy—I realize who he is, now. Not Erich Manh Coelm, but—

He sees me in the mirror and smiles. "Was it good for you too, baby?"

I rush forward, fear or no fear, and grasp at him with my clawed hand, but he catches my wrist and pulls it around my back. I struggle, but he's just too strong.

"Now, now," he says. "Is that any way to treat an old friend?"

Claws clicking, I glare over my shoulder at him. "Tearing the rest of your face off, EMC? That's just neighborly, is what that is."

"Heh, cute."

He shoves me away, into the center of the bathroom. I crouch, ready to spring, but he pulls out a hand cannon to point at me. Shit.

"Oh sure, big EMC, hiding behind a gun. As usual."

His face draws into an annoyed glower. "It's $E = MC^2$. Like the equation? You know."

"Whatever."

"Really, V." He sneers, content in his own superiority. "I'm kind of surprised you didn't get it earlier, but then again smarts have never been your thing. Still." He slips out a business card—the same one he gave me. He sets it on the counter so I can read it. "I would have thought *Erich Manh Coelm* was a dead give-away."

"The initials?"

EMC frowns. "It's an anagram?"

"Anagram?"

"For my real name?" he says. "Emil March Cohen."

"Fuck, you have a *real* name?"

"Antagonizing the guy with the gun? Now *that's* the chutzpah I remember."

He isn't kidding. His gun looks more like a loudspeaker, encircled with copper wires that crackle with electricity. Damn tech savants.

"The insolence is sexy, but it's a bit ungrateful after all I've done for you."

"Done for me?" I ask. "I—"

Then I remember, even with my head being all fuzzy.

My mind flashes back to a few hours to the bar, when Coelm came back for his flask. How he apologized, and how he looked so cute in his contrition. How we flirted a little more . . .

I remember the rest of it, too, which really was quite good.

I hadn't been drugged—just drunk and stupid enough to sleep with a super-villain. Typical, really.

"Still, liquor and bathroom sex?" I ask. "Kind of kinky, eh, EMC? What would your mother say?"

"I *told* you, it's—look, whatever."

I remember him: a poor man's Big-Head—crazy/smart thinking machine, human super-computer, gone over to Villainy™. Can't remember much about him, except that I gave him those three scars on his cheek, and I can picture a series of various members of Supergroup punching him in the face. Never gets old.

I come at EMC again, with a move the Raven taught me back in the day, but he's ready for it. He doesn't shoot the gun, but instead catches me and slams me hard into the row of sinks.

"Look at yourself," he says. His free hand wrenches my head up. "No really—look."

I look in the mirror: jet-black hair, wine-colored eyes, familiar nose and cheeks. The me in the mirror wears way too much makeup—

black lipstick, way too much eye shadow, liner that twists to her temples. She's me, as a goth girl, a phase I got over twenty years ago.

"My god," I say. "Did you dress me up in a Halloween knock-off of my old costume? That's a new low, even for you."

"No, look again," EMC says. "I did this all for you, you know."

I look closer, and now I see what he means. It's me, sure—but the goth girl in the mirror can't be more than twenty-five. She isn't a grown woman dressed up like a kid. She *is* a kid.

"Fuck," I say. "How'd you do that?"

He raised the gun level with my head. "Retro-Active Molecular Modification Electro-Repulsor." He beams. "I call it RAMMER."

"Compensating," I murmur.

"Anyway," he says. "Anything I blast with it retrogrades in time, becoming an immature version of itself. Takes a bitter soccer mom like yourself and makes her a hot, dark super-heroine—you know, like you were twenty years ago. You know, when we first met and I fell in love with you."

"Oh," I say. "*Oh.*" I lean closer to examine my twenty-something self. "Wow."

"Totally cool, right?" He presses his lips to my ear, his breath hot on my skin. "Not to mention you make love like you look, baby."

"Mmm," I say, pursing my lips. "You know what else I do like I look?"

"Uh—?"

"Hit."

I head-butt him in the nose, sending him staggering. Then—when I wheel around and kick him in the junk—he slumps to the floor.

"Really? 'Make love'?" I say over him. "Who says that?"

As he coughs, I narrow my eyes, focusing on absorbing his fear, but again there's just that empty haze. Some kind of power-blocking device—the sort that technosavants love. With my luck, it's even built to fuck with my powers in particular. Son of a bitch.

The distraction lets him recover enough to point the retro-thingy at me, and I hoof it to the door. He fires, a crazy *wazza-pow!* sort of sound, and a jet of rainbow energy shoots past me and hits a poster on the wall. It shrivels and swirls and becomes an advertisement for an AC/DC concert. Woah.

I stagger out into the hall, heels clicking as I go—why the hell did I ever put heels on my costume?—and look both ways. We're in an airport terminal, completely abandoned—no planes arrived at any of the gates. Muzak gently wafts from the speakers at the corners of the walls. Lightning flashes out the windows—the storm's even worse.

Signs say Terminal D, which makes sense: I vaguely remember a sign that said "Terminal D under renovation." Where better to hide out, if you're a super-villain?

No map, so one direction is as good as another. I go right, looking for somewhere to hide. Preferably somewhere with—ah. A white courtesy phone.

I pick the phone off the wall, check it for a dial tone—yes!—and hide around the wall. I don't see EMC, but he can't be too far. I've got maybe thirty seconds.

I don't call the cops—they might as well be the boys in red (shirts) for this sort of thing—and I don't call Andre ('cuz honestly, what's he gonna do?). I certainly don't call the Raven, since I'm not that desperate. Instead, I take out the business card I swiped off the table and flip it over. Marcus's digits are neatly printed on the back.

"Time for an old-school team-up," I murmur, and dial the number into the phone.

There's a ring, and a click, and a voice speaks up, in my ear and over the loudspeaker. "Hello, Lady V," EMC says.

My heart sinks. "Fuck you," I announce.

There's a wazza-zap, and a burst of rainbow light turns the white courtesy phone into something Alexander Graham Bell would have been ashamed for people to see. Another hit from that retro-ray thing, and I'm gonna be what, a toddler? Fuck that.

I drop the 19$^{th}$ century ringer and run around the corner, even as the tall, good-looking asshole comes rushing up, retro-gun at the ready.

The loudspeakers buzz. "Paging Lady Vengeance," a man's voice says. "Lady Vengeance, please meet your party at *you're gonna fuckin' die, bitch!*"

I duck, and an unused computer monitor becomes a TV best suited for Technicolor.

He chases me into the food court, which is really the only place I can go to hide. It's central, and I can go either of two ways. Also, plenty of tables to absorb the retro-gun fire. I stay low and zigzag, looking for an exit. Unfortunately, I see EMC first, and I dive over the counter of a fast-food burger joint. One blast from the retro-gun, and the storefront becomes the classic golden arches, complete with deep fat fryers bubbling.

I could keep running, but not for long. Time for another strategy.

"Do you like the costume?" he asks loudly, his voice coming closer. He's taking his time, taunting me—or flirting. I can't tell. "I bought it, you know—the original."

What's most impressive is that he found the original, after I gave it to the Salvation Army fifteen years ago. Either that, or he's fucking with me.

"It still smelled like you, but not quite the same. I just had to see it on you again."

What a perv.

EMC's face appears over the counter, and I hurl a batch of fries in his face. Grease spatters and he ducks. His aim goes wild. The retro-gun sprays, and a glass sculpture in the middle of the food court turns into a knock-off statue of David.

"Hai!" I shout, slashing at his wrist. I might have been tempted to go for the face, but one blast of that Retro-gun thing would put me back into diapers (or worse, a cat suit), and that'd be that.

Whether he was bullshitting me about the original costume or not, the claws are sharp. I cut his wrist so deeply his hand nearly comes off.

There's no blood, however, nor does he look pained—just mildly irked. His arm ends in a clean cut, like silicon more than flesh.

Fucking techno-savants.

We stare at one another—him without a hand, me staring at his disembodied hand on the floor. The retro-gun lies on the floor between us.

"Come on, baby," he says. "I didn't mean to piss you off. You were just on my list."

"List?" I ask. "What list?"

"Ten things to do before I retire," EMC says. "You were number nine."

"Number nine," I say. "Me."

"Have you seen yourself in that costume? *Damn!*" he says. "I mean, the only thing that could make it better is if you hit me a couple times first—you know, for old time's sake."

"Eww," I say.

"And now that I've taken care of number nine, I can move onto number ten—world domination," he explains. "With my RAMMER technology, I can devolve any technology anyone sends against me until it's obsolete. No one can stand against me! No one!" He throws back his head and laughs. Then he looks at me. "Thanks, incidentally."

"Don't mention it—I mean *really*."

I go for it, but he's faster. I am, after all, a little drunk.

"Such a shame," he says, pointing the gun at my face. "I needed a queen of the world, but you're just a little too stubborn. Maybe a younger you will go for it."

The gun charges up with a whine.

An arrow streaks out of nowhere and hits EMC in the shoulder, spoiling his aim. He falls, and his retro-gun turns an airport cart into a red tricycle.

I look over, and there's Marcus, gold armor shining under his coat, a bow in his hands. He's got a second arrow ready. "Drop it!" he shouts.

EMC does what all villains do when backed into a corner. He goes for it.

I catch the gun, rip it out of his hands, and whip him across the face with the barrel. He drops like a stone.

Marcus—the Huntsman—strides up to me, arrow trained on EMC's face. "Are you OK, Lady V?" he asks. "Did he—woah."

"What?" I ask, but instantly I get it. I hold up the gun. "Retro-thing."

"You're—you're *you*," he says. "I mean, the old you. I mean, the younger you—"

"Careful with the jaw, kid," I say. "It's hanging out."

He shuts his mouth, but he's still smiling.

"How'd you get the call anyway?" I ask. "I thought EMC diverted it."

"Oh, the Protectorate has this thing, where if anyone dials that number, we get an alert."

"Slick."

"Baby—" EMC's head twitches abruptly to one side. "Baby number nine—baby—"

"So, uh, what's up with him?" Marcus asks.

Sparks shoot out of EMC's mouth. I should have known.

"Broke my damn rule," I murmur.

"Huh?"

I aim the retro-gun at EMC and pull the trigger. He warps, swirls, then becomes first a computer, then a wind-up toy, then a toaster.

"Robot," I explain.

"Oh," he says. "So where's the real . . .?"

Lightning flashes outside the terminal, and warning sirens sound. Beams of rainbow light shoot out like lightning. One strikes a plane taxiing down the runway, and it abruptly becomes a propjet. A baggage cart becomes a VW bus painted with flowers.

We look out at the chaos on the airfield, then look up at its source—the unused flight control tower. We nod to one another, totally on the same page.

"Hey," I say. "Can you conjure up that dark woman again?"

"You mean the Queen of the Black Sigh?" He shudders.

"Cool name for an archvillain." I can feel his fear coiling. "And yep, that oughta do it."

We don't bother with the stairs—probably wired with explosives or machine guns anyway. Instead, we burst right up through the floor of the control tower, me slugging through the concrete, Marcus ready with the bow right after.

The tower looks like your standard technosavant's evil lair: Matrix knock-off with wires hanging down, computer monitors all over, and shivering robot guards waiting by the exits.

We take them by surprise, and it's pretty much a massacre worthy of Michael Bay. The kid's pretty good with that bow, plus he keeps feeding me one of the sweetest fears I've ever tasted: this Queen of the Black Sigh thing. And he doesn't even collapse in moaning terror every time he sees me, which is a plus. I can't imagine how terrible his fear might once have been, and how powerful it would make me if I drank that one.

*Stop that, V,* I tell myself. *And stop calling him the kid—you're all of five minutes older than him, at this point.*

"Where is he?" Marcus asks, just before a beam of rainbow light bursts from the retro-gun in my hand, arcs around, and hits him. He mouths a silent cry and falls to the floor, shifting—turning into something before his time.

And as he goes down, so too departs the fear giving me power. I become myself: a twenty-something, heavily made up goth girl, who brought claws to a retro-gun fight.

The real EMC appears, and at his wave, the gun rips free of my hand and tosses itself over to him. This is more like the evil genius I remember: small, lanky except for a beer belly, and with the crazy silver hair that destines him for anything but management. Also, he's older than I was even when I was the older me. What a creep.

"Hey baby," he says, in a voice like that of the robot but higher-pitched. He flexes his nerd muscles. "Like what you see?"

"Seriously *eww,*" I say.

"Be that as it may," he says. "I knew you wouldn't like this body—that's why I made the other one. He's Raven, Justice, and me— an amalgam of all the men you ever wanted—"

"Plus you," I say.

He glowers at me. "And obviously married too, because I know you're a slut like that."

"You are such a dick," I say.

"Yes, but I know your type, don't I?" The retro-gun is whining, powering up. "I've clearly won, and there's nothing you can do about it now. Noth—"

He's really getting to a good villainous monologue—I can see it building—but unfortunately for him, an arrow scythes up from the floor and splits the retro-gun in two neat halves. Rainbow lightning arcs from it in all directions, and EMC's eyes go wide.

"No, no!" he cries.

The blast strikes him, and he shifts. The mad scientist gives way to a rich bald guy with a sneer, then to an old English gentlemen with an "M" on his handkerchief, then to a Shakespearean nobleman with a gimpy leg. Then he disappears entirely—vanished into the depths of a literary gap, where evil geniuses haven't been invented yet.

The retro-gun falls, smoking, to the floor.

I look over, and there's the Huntsman kneeling on the ground at my feet. Something about him seems odd, though—familiar in a way Marcus had never been. Darker.

"You OK?" I ask.

"I think," he says in a deeper, cooler voice. "I think I'm my *father.*"

"Now *that* is fucked," I say, and cross to the sparking retro-gun. I pick it up gingerly, and raise it over my head to slam against the floor.

He puts his hand on my arm. "Wait," he says, in a commanding way that I obey instantly. "I—my father—"

I understand. I can feel it, in the fear coursing through him—that this might be his best chance to learn about a father he didn't really know. And that's something I can definitely relate to. I feel it too, the old Huntsman's fear—not Marcus's. It isn't the one Marcus expects, oddly enough. It tells me that what he thinks about his father isn't quite true.

I smile wanly. "Don't worry." I touch his cheek lightly with my black-gloved fingers. "Everything's going to be all right."

I raise the retro-gun in both hands once more.

"Are you sure about this, V?" he asks. "If breaking that undoes everything, won't you go back to . . . the way you were?"

"What's wrong with the way I was?" I flash him one of my wry grins—an expression that hasn't faded much from when my age matched my body. "Besides the bitterness, the regrets, and the alcoholic tendencies?"

"Huh," he says. "When you put it that way . . ."

I smash the damned thing into a thousand clanging pieces of shrapnel.

At first, nothing happens. We're still in a retro paradise, and still retro versions of ourselves. Then suddenly I'm older. Every birthday comes to pass in the span of five seconds. My joints stiffen, my liver aches—but at least I'm me again.

EMC reappears, sliding back into reality from babyhood. I look away, having seen quite enough naked mad scientist for one night.

And Marcus—well, he becomes *Marcus*. A different Huntsman—younger, fresher, and with a whole new life ahead of him.

"Wow," he says. "That—that really was a team-up, wasn't it?"

I shrug.

The storm passes, and even at this distance, I can see the other terminal whirring back to life. The sun is rising, and it's a new day.

"Well, got a plane to catch," I say, looking at my watch. Then I lean in and kiss him on the cheek. "Look me up in about ten years, kid."

As Marcus's face goes red, I swagger off into the sunrise, black cape flapping, thinking only one thing:

*Dear God, I hope the GAP is open this early.*

# TIMESLIP

**Erik Scott de Bie.** *Erik Scott de Bie likes villains--especially super-villains, and even more especially super-villains-turned-heroes. His character, Lady Vengeance is one such: a hero with villainous powers who isn't afraid to get her hands dirty. She stars in a comic book he plans to write one day. One with lots of drinking. When not writing about awesome dark ladies and exactly how much butt they kick, Erik spends time with his wife and cats in Seattle. He is the author of numerous works of fiction both long and short, including the novels* Ghostwalker, Depths of Madness, *and* Downshadow *in the Forgotten Realms setting. His next novel,* Shadowbane, *is due out in September 2011.*

# TIMESLIP

## Girl's Night Out
### 1935

Imp had been in worse situations with her long-time companion, Devil Cat, but she couldn't think of any right away. At moments like this, she cared less about her own safety compared with her partner's. He was driven by a sense of justice, she by a desire to keep him out of trouble. The last of the Martin Magoo gang stood at the edge of the Quayside rooftop, cornered by the Diabolical Duo. The stench of the river wafted through the air to them, a mix of sewage and chemicals. The summer heat only made the smell worse.

The six thugs readied for the fight. Some cracked their knuckles, others waved the improvised weapons they had scavenged in their attempt to escape. Imp didn't doubt that she and Devil Cat could win, but this would be a long, ugly fight.

Devil Cat, the crime-fighting alter ego of wealthy socialite Thomas Carlton, cocked the hammers on his matching custom Tokarev TT-30s. He wore a black suit and tie, blood-red dress shirt, fedora and a dark red half mask shaped to look like a cat. Imp, who was known in other circles as Carlton's faithful companion Grace Glass, adopted a fighting stance she had learned in the Orient. She wore a man's burgundy suit and black domino mask. They exchanged a brief look, each knowing how to best approach this situation to complement the other's abilities.

An explosion ripped the air behind them, almost knocking Imp off of her feet. She turned just in time to see a sled sliding past where Devil Cat had been standing. Sparks flew as it scraped along the rooftop and left a smoking trail of scorched tarpaper. Imp coughed and covered her nose against the pungent smoke. The streamlined nose had caught Devil Cat, who had rolled over the top and into the body of the vehicle. The Magoo gang scattered like bowling pins as the sled careened towards them. It took out a chunk of the parapet and tumbled off the edge of the building.

"Oh, for the love of Pete!" Imp exclaimed.

Instead of falling, the vehicle pulled upward sharply. The sled was the size of a skiff, with baroque ornamentation along the sides. On either side were large blue crystalline boulders that smoldered in the dark of the night. In the sled, an almost naked man was struggling with several metal automatons. A similarly clad woman clung to the edge of the sled as it bobbed up and down in the air. At the prow of the vehicle, she could see Devil Cat pulling himself into the sled.

Imp glanced back at the source of the original sound and saw a circle in the air ten feet back that showed a desert landscape spreading off into the distance. A cold wind blew from the circle, carrying with it the smells of cinnamon and sand.

She turned her attention back to the departing sled. It caught the edge of the rooftop across the street. It bucked in the air at the impact, tossing the woman from the vehicle. The man tried to race to the edge of the flying skiff but found his way blocked by the robots. The woman didn't scream as she fell. She grabbed a window ledge to stop her descent before pressing herself up with just her arms and swinging her leg up to the window ledge.

"Um, Miss Imp?" someone said.

In her distraction, Imp had forgotten the Magoo gang was still there. One of the goons stood a safe distance away, his hands raised and his face ashen with fear.

"What?" she asked in exasperation. The sled was slowly disappearing off to the east. Regency Heights? Why would robots be taking a flying sled to the wealthiest part of the city?

"We give up. Just don' throw no more of those flyin' things at us."

"Good. Stay here until I get back."

The goon nodded and sat down on the rooftop. His peers followed suit. Imp ran back to the roof entrance, skirting the circle in the air at a safe distance. By the time she had run back down to the ground floor, across the street and back up the stairs of the next building, she was starting to feel winded. It had been a long night and didn't promise to get any shorter.

Imp kicked in the door of the office she estimated was behind the window to which the other woman had been clinging. As the door burst inward, someone jumped back to avoid being hit. It was the woman from the sled. The other woman was clad in a skimpy outfit consisting of a leather harness decorated with jewels and feathers. Quick as lightning, the woman raised a strange-looking pistol like a shard of red crystal with brass coiled about it and aimed it at Imp.

Without hesitation, Imp closed the distance to raise the other woman's gun arm up so that the shot would hit the ceiling. As part of the same forward motion, she swept the other woman's legs. What Imp didn't expect was for the woman to grab her by the sleeve and pull Imp down with her.

As the two fell, the gun went off. A jagged beam of light shot from the front of the pistol and carved a burning line down the face of one wall. The smell of ozone and scorched plaster filled the air. Imp twisted as they landed, using her momentum to drive her elbow into the stranger's ribs. The other woman let out a grunt of pain. While the almost naked woman was distracted, Imp twisted the woman's arm until she dropped the gun.

The other woman swung her leg up and kicked Imp from behind, which caused Devil Cat's companion to stumble forward. Imp turned just in time to see the other woman spring from her supine position up to her feet in a single quick motion before turning to face Imp in a defensive stance.

Imp didn't recognize the style, but given the hole she had seen in the world she wasn't too surprised.

"I suppose it's pointless to ask what happened to Devil Cat," Imp said, settling into her own defensive posture.

"You speak English?" the woman asked. Her voice was deep and throaty with a thick accent.

"You seem surprised."

"I learned it from the only other person I have known to that speak that tongue. I nearly thought he made it up."

"And who was it that taught you?"

"In my world he is Sakar-To, Prince of the Wastes and Admiral of the Air Fleet of Promethium. The name he used before coming to our world was Philip Fletcher of the City of Cobalt."

"Do you mean Cobalt City?"

"I suppose that is another way to say it."

"What a funny coincidence." Imp sighed. "Welcome to Cobalt City. So who are you and what brings you to our fair New England town?"

"New England," the strange woman said, contemplating the words. "Another name I have only heard of in tales from my beloved. To answer your questions, my name is Princess Melet-Dar of Promethium. Our airship was stolen by mechanical men while we were in it. While my beloved Sakar-To sought to retake the ship, the men activated a device which tore a gate to your city."

"Then your Sakar-To has been taken to wherever your airship went?"

"That would appear to be a safe conclusion."

"My partner was on the same ship last I saw it, and he probably needs my help. Care to work together to deal with the machine men that stole your airship?"

"That seems like an excellent notion," Melet-Dar said as she relaxed from her fighting stance.

"Great! Now, before we go out hunting stolen airships we may want to get you some... well, clothes."

The Alfa Romeo 8C raced down the late night streets of Cobalt City. The car was painted black, with subtle use of dark red to suggest the image of a devilish feline predator on the hood. Behind the wheel, Imp scanned the eastern skies for any further sign of the airship that had carried away Devil Cat.

Beside her sat Melet-Dar, wearing the spare shirt and trousers that Imp kept in the trunk in case of emergency. Imp's plan had been to provide the Promethian princess with enough clothing to prevent her from being arrested for indecency. Imp hadn't expected Melet-Dar to strip her clothing off in the middle of the street before putting on the local attire. The street Imp had parked on was empty, so the jacket she held up in front of the princess ended up doing little more than preserving Imp's sense of decorum.

"How did someone from our world make it into yours?" Imp asked, breaking the silence. The car smelled of strange and alien spices that Imp could not identify. She assumed it was the princess from another world.

"He ran afoul of a scientist at one point," Melet-Dar said. "Or a thief, depending on how you look at it. His name was Doctor Kindred and he had stolen some sort of technology from a race that travels from world to world. Sakar-To had tried to stop him, and the world-traveling device exploded. When Sakar-To awoke again, he was in Promethium."

"What rare fortune he is still alive," Imp said.

"What of this Devil Cat? Is he your beloved?"

"Not exactly," Imp replied, focusing harder at the street ahead of her.

"What is it, 'exactly?'"

"Complicated," Imp said, hedging further.

"Is he married?"

"No."

"Pining over a lost love?"

"No."

"Interested in men?"

"What? No."

"Then I do not understand the complication."

"We've talked about it. What we do, going out and trying to fight crime. It's very high risk, so it's hard to commit to someone when you could die at any time."

"I think that is the ideal time to commit to someone," Melet-Dar huffed. "Were this the last day of your life, would you really want to waste it in hesitation?"

"I wouldn't even know where to begin to change his mind," Imp began to explain.

"I have found it quite effective to enter their chambers at night, clad in only a robe and nothing underneath. Once you unpin your hair and drop your robe, he should—"

Imp slammed on the brakes.

Ahead of them on the road a small crowd was gathered around something on the ground. Some turned and raised their hands against the glare of the headlights. The two women got out of the car and approached the crowd, which parted before them. The tone of the conversation shifted as people recognized Imp.

In the middle of the group was a prone body, its limbs shattered by the fall. It still twitched feebly, as though trying to find the will to live. Sparks twitched off of it every few seconds and it reeked of burning plastic.

"That looks like one of the robots that were on your sled," Imp pointed out.

"So it would appear," Melet-Dar agreed.

Turning to the crowd Imp asked, "Did any of you see where the flying craft this fell from went?"

A boy of about ten stepped forward and pointed further east. "I saw some more of those things fall off of it as it flew past."

"It's like they've left us a trail of cookie crumbs to follow," Imp said.

Without wasting time, the pair ran off into the night. Before long, they came across a second robot that had fallen and shattered the ornamental fountain on a mansion's front lawn. Further on they saw a third impaled on the spikes topping a wrought iron fence. The last one they found was in the middle of the lawn of a sprawling estate. The feet stuck straight up from the ground, kicking feebly.

Melet-Dar knelt down to examine the robot. "It appears that there is some sort of hatch hidden within this ornamental foliage. I am not certain how to open it."

"Can you cut it open with that zap gun of yours?"

"Perhaps, but I do not want to waste the charge on that. I am confident that there is an alternate point of entry."

"Let's check out the mansion," Imp suggested.

As they stepped up to the front door, Imp moved to press the doorbell.

"What are you doing?" Melet-Dar asked before Imp could touch it.

"I thought it would at least be civil to ring the bell, in case the people living in the house are not connected with the robots."

"What about the element of surprise?"

Just as the princess said that, the trap door opened beneath their feet.

The two women explored their environment in darkness for a few minutes before a bright light illuminated the area. They were in a small stone cell with one wall made of glass. A man stood on the other side of the glass, regarding them.

He was in his forties, stocky build, with a mane of once-dark hair turned to gray and a matching goatee. He was clad in a well-tailored English drape cut suit. His expression was a mix of annoyance and boredom.

"Trespassing, are we?"

"We were going to ring your doorbell just as you sprung your trap," Imp clarified.

"How civil of you."

"Are you responsible for the machine men?" Melet-Dar asked.

"Why yes," he said with a proud smile. "Those would be mine."

"And your name?"

"Doctor Kindred," the man replied.

"The thief who sent Phillip Fletcher to another world?" Imp asked.

"Oh. You're with him. To be honest, I thought I had killed him. As for being a thief, I should point out that I have broken no city, state or federal laws, little lady."

"You stole from the royal family of Promethium," Melet-Dar pointed out.

"And yet there are no extradition treaties between the United States and Promethium. A shame that."

"But kidnapping is a crime." Imp cracked her knuckles. "You don't really think a little bit of glass will keep me from giving you a good thrashing, do you?"

"Why, yes. I do. This is a sophisticated composite of my own design—"

Melet-Dar fired her gun at the window, tracing a circle in the surface and leaving a trail of molten glass behind. Glowering at the doctor as he backed up in alarm, she strode forward and kicked out the disk from the window with her sandaled foot.

As the doctor turned and ran, he pulled a control box out of his pocket and pressed a few buttons. By the time Imp and the princess climbed through the hole, a wave of automata came charging at them.

The two women battled upstream through the horde, Melet-Dar scything through them with her ray gun while Imp used the robots' momentum to spin them into one another. They burst through the lines of defense with a few straggling machines following in their wake.

Beyond the corridor was a vast underground laboratory. The smell of ozone and chemicals permeated the air. Hanging over a vat of a bubbling orange liquid were Devil Cat and Sakar-To, their wrists manacled and attached to the ceiling. On the far side of the lab was the skiff, with an elaborate array of devices surrounding the crystals on the sides of it.

"What have you boys gotten up to now?" Imp called out.

"Just catching up with my old friend Philip," Devil Cat replied. "We went to college together, can you believe that?"

"And here I was worried about you," Imp said.

"You should be worried," Doctor Kindred called out from a catwalk above them. "Do you think someone who has managed to travel through the Coil of worlds is someone to be trifled with?"

"You only travel through worlds with technology you stole," said Sakar-To.

"On the contrary," said the scientist. "I had to reconstruct that device after it had exploded, reverse engineering the technology in order to produce multiple units."

"But what would you do with such technology?" Imp asked.

"I'm glad you asked," Doctor Kindred said with a smile. He cleared his throat and adjusted his jacket. "I have been seeking out more technologically advanced worlds in order to obtain their technology and turn it to my own profit. If you'll give me a moment, I have a chart that will illustrate my larger plan—"

"I've heard of villains who like to monologue, but this is taking it a bit far," Devil Cat said, struggling at his bonds.

Doctor Kindred glanced at his watch. "Well, you've caught me. I was stalling for time while my death trap reaches full capacity. I have deduced how to resonate the power crystals from the air skiff so that they will explode. That combined with the chemicals stored here will kill you all. I merely wanted to delay you in order to make your death more likely. You can try to flee for your lives, but I do not give you good odds of that."

"Would you not die as well?" Melet-Dar asked.

The doctor opened his shirt to reveal a clockwork mechanism. "I am already miles away. Really, did you think I would be standing here mocking you in the flesh when there is a violent alien princess with a ray gun running around?"

The princess fired off a beam of energy at the doppelganger's head, causing it to shatter and burn.

"He was boring me," Melet-Dar explained when Imp looked at her in surprise. "Do we have a plan for getting them down in time to exit this lair before the crystals explode?"

"Will the skiff still fly if the crystals are about to explode?" Imp asked.

"Yes, but it will accelerate the process."

Without further commentary, Imp made a dash for the sled. Melet-Dar followed right behind her.

"How do I fly this thing?" Imp asked as she vaulted over the railing of the sled.

"You don't," the princess responded. "This is a sophisticated piece of Promethian military hardware. It would take months of training in order to attain basic competency."

"Yes, but I need you to shoot out the manacles holding the men while I fly this," Imp explained as she pulled a lever. The sled lurched to the side with the sound of twisting metal.

Melet-Dar clutched the railing in wide-eyed surprise. "This was not how I planned on dying."

"Really? I hadn't really planned that far. How about we put that off until after we get out of here?"

The princess muttered an expletive in her native language before giving basic instructions on the controls. The sled tore free from its moorings and careened towards the two captive men. As the sled passed between the prisoners and the vat, the princess fired her gun at the manacles and the men dropped to the sled. The railing of the sled caught Sakar-To in the ribs. This was exacerbated when Devil Cat landed on top of his old school chum.

"What is your plan for getting us out of here?" Devil Cat asked.

"I didn't think to figure out how to open the hatch in Kindred's lawn," Imp said. "So I'm going to try and go back the way we came."

Imp's three passengers turned to look towards the front of the sled just as it plunged into the corridor. The crystals on the sides of the sled sparked as they skidded along the walls, shedding exploding fragments as it went.

"Watch your heads and hold on!" Imp called out, just as she turned sharply and broke through the glass of the prison she was in earlier.

She twisted the controls so that the nose pointed up towards the trap door, and accelerated rapidly.

The nose of the sled burst through the trap door and then stopped abruptly. It was wedged into the small entry, the crystals on the sides too big to fit through. The four passengers looked around and, on seeing that they were outside, scrambled off the sled and ran through the yard. They reached the fence just as the building behind them exploded into green and purple flame.

The four of them waited for the police to arrive. The Commissioner himself showed up, staring wide-eyed at the conflagration of the mansion. The heat was intense, warming all of their faces. Within minutes, the group had briefed the Commissioner on the night's events.

"Doctor Kindred a villain!" the Commissioner exclaimed. "Why, I was at one of his dinner parties just last month. To think that a robot laboratory was under my feet the whole time!"

At that statement, the lawn collapsed in a fiery display.

"Hopefully you won't judge our city by the events of tonight," the Commissioner said. "Not everyone in this city is a mad scientist looking to steal airships."

"I assure you my opinion of your city is unmarred," Melet-Dar replied. Imp was amazed that the same woman who had fought at her side earlier that evening now behaved like the noble that her title would suggest. Even in scorched, secondhand clothes, she looked like royalty. From the adoration in Sakar-To's eyes, on the other hand, it was clear he thought of her more as a goddess.

"You'll be happy to know, Devil Cat, that the Magoo gang is under lock and key. They came along meek as lambs."

"Good to know, Commissioner. You can thank Imp for that. I was indisposed."

"Well done, little lady!"

"It just took a little fear of the Devil to keep them in line."

"We really should get going," Sakar-To said. "I'm not sure how long that portal will remain and it's really best if we returned as soon as possible."

A short, if cramped, ride in the Alfa Romeo brought them back to the Quayside building where the trouble had began. While climbing the stairs, Sakar-To said, "You're welcome to come with us. Promethium could use more people like you."

"It's tempting," Devil Cat replied. "But I'm dedicated to protecting this city. And I'm awfully fond of wearing actual clothes."

Sakar-To laughed and continued bantering with Devil Cat while Melet-Dar hooked Imp's arm and fell back a few steps behind the men.

"You could have died back there," the princess pointed out.

"So could you," Imp said. "But we didn't."

"Yet I would have gone to my grave without any regrets."

Imp opened her mouth to say something then snapped it shut. She focused her gaze forward and was silent the rest of the hike up the stairs.

"It's smaller than it was earlier," Imp pointed out as they arrived on the roof. The circle in the air was half the size it once was.

"Then I guess we had better hurry," Sakar-To said.

Melet-Dar looked pointedly at Imp without saying anything.

"Fine, you were right," Imp sighed.

The princess smiled and embraced the masked martial artist. "Good luck."

The four of them said farewell to one another before the warrior and the princess jumped through the hole between worlds.

"What were the two of you talking about back there?" Devil Cat asked.

"Oh, girl talk. Nothing that would interest you," Imp said with a smirk.

"Ah."

"But now that we are alone, I have a few things I'd like to talk to you about."

*Jeremy Zimmerman's passion is for games and storytelling. His writing for games has been published by such companies as Guardians of Order and Goodman Games. His fiction can be found in Crossed Genres and Wily Writers. He lives in Seattle with his girlfriend and five bossy cats. More info can be found at his Web site www.bolthy.com.*

# TIMESLIP

Jax...

My name is Jax...

*Merde.* Today does not feel like a good day to be me.

Groaning, I get to my feet and stagger towards the sound of running water. Drinking the clean icy stream shocks me into greater awareness but the disorientation's fierce. Rich arboreal scents of a New England forest, but they're too clean, and the trees too large. The quality of light seems wrong, more autumn than summer.

I look down. My befuddled face stares back at me from the cupped pool in my hands, my normally mahogany eyes looking more like twice-glazed walnuts.

*<the sword...>*

Knowledge slices through me, my reflected face shattering on the mossy rocks. I'm not in 2012 anymore. Oh hell, it worked... it really worked. I'm pretty sure I even survived.

Why, oh why, does time-travel have to hurt like a motherfucker? I mean, really. The blinding light I understand. The rushing wind makes sense. The taste of strawberries... well, that's just odd, but I can roll with it. It's the bone-grinding, skin-boiling, blood-shattering pain that seems just plain excessive.

*<The Sword...>*

If I'd developed a time-travel machine, it would have a feature set that did NOT include both "compelling chrononaut's stomach to invert itself" as well as "confessing sins never before conceived of in some vain hope for supernatural absolution and anesthetization". To wit, the toad in front of me remains unimpressed with what I never did to my fictional wife's dachshund.

# TIMESLIP

## *<The Sword...>*

Damnit! Okay, I hear you... me... whatever! Never did care for post-hypnotic implants. They itch like mad inside my head but shaking it, a very natural reaction, doesn't dislodge anything useful... and almost calls up an encore performance from my stomach. Okay, right, need to calm down and relax into this. Heart rate's up and breathing's too shallow. Time to lie down, close my eyes, breathe deeply, and let my training kick in. Not that different from solving a Rubik's cube, actually.

## *<T-H-E S-W-O-R-D...>*

Honestly, why no "snooze" option on these implants? Sigh. On my third breath I finally forget my body and trigger the insistent memory.

The onslaught is abrupt and fierce as I fast forward through every memory and sensation I've ever experienced. Many people have claimed envy over my talent to learn and memorize; information as well as physical skills. But this means perfect recall of pain as well as pleasure, failure as well as success, horror as well as divinity... well, it's hard to explain the exquisite agony of orange paisley bell-bottoms to someone born blind.

The exception here is language, which is pure joy. Each new language reinvents my world with the vibrancy of a new lover. It's why I prefer exotic field jobs like this, emphasizing languages and physical skills, over desk-assignments with the constant intellectual cud chewing.

Ah... there we go...

Through childhood's wonder-filled frustrations, my teenaged majestic angst, and early adulthood's rollercoaster, I spill into a mental clearing with the post-hypnotic seed. Slowly revolving in my mind's eye is the upright sword of the Avalon Group, my employer. Mentally grasping the hilt, I feel the remaining tendrils of time-traveler's jet lag sheared off with yesterday's memory... 425 years in the future...

Cobalt City's midday sun warms my cheek through high-rise office windows. Air-conditioning mitigates the summer heat and carries a subtle taste of rosemary. My silk shirt glides along my shoulders as I turn from urban bustle below to the distant green of Lafayette Park. A flush of suppressed excitement dusts my cheeks while my fingers trail over the Avalon Group's embossed logo, the upright sword, and open the dossier folder with my next assignment: the Occultus Vox of Lafayette Park.

> **Mission Portfolio**: *Untitled*
> **Security Level:** *Ascension Rites/Discretion III*
> **Domain**: *North America – United States – Cobalt City*
> **Target**: *Cobalt City*
> **Fiscal Year** *(Quarter): 2012 (Q4)*
> **Supervisor in Charge** *(SiC): Z. Harrison, Chevalier du Pique*
> **Agent in Charge** *(AiC): Jax, Valet du Pique*
> **Objectives:*1) Field test new time-travel device. 2) Find William Wythers. 3) Gather detailed accounting of all actions and actors in the establishment of the Lafayette Park Occultus Vox.*

Well, hurrah for me, objective 1 is already done.

<Flip>

**Keys:** *1) William Wythers. Born 1570, Devonshire, England. Landed with the second Roanoke Colony in 1587. He is the only confirmed individual present and part of the inception event for this Occultus Vox (O.V.), circa 1587. Exact function in event remains unknown. 2) Sword of Sophia. Major artifact originating in 13$^{th}$ century Jerusalem and presumed intrinsic to the survival of Ordo Templari into the modern day. The hand-and-a-half sword is distinguished by scrollwork on the blade and Sophia's emblem of a dove crowned in stars etched on the cross-guard. Last known in possession of the Wythers family in Devonshire, considered integral to the familial heritage.*

<Flip>

**Background**: *Though affected by numerous natural disasters since its founding in 1723, Cobalt City always suffers significantly less damage than surrounding areas. In 1984, the Avalon Group's thaumaturgical survey revealed several aberrant and densely magical concentrations*

*(known as "Occultus Vox" or "O.V.") with varying relationships to the
city. Current research indicates that attunement to the Lafayette Park
O.V. is critical to Avalon Group's satisfaction of primary stakeholder
needs. Current research further indicates that any attunement attempts
require explicit details of individual O.V. inception; including full
context of artifact usage and individual actions/emotions.* ▮▮▮▮▮▮

▮▮▮▮▮▮▮▮▮▮▮▮▮▮▮▮▮▮▮▮▮▮▮▮▮▮▮▮▮▮▮▮▮▮▮▮

<Flip>

**Additional Notes:**
*"Jax, I want to be excruciatingly clear on this. This action will eventually
be visible all the way up to the Chair of the Board, the Green Mother,
herself. She wants* ▮▮▮▮▮▮▮▮▮▮▮▮▮▮▮▮▮▮
▮▮▮▮▮▮▮▮▮▮▮▮▮▮▮▮▮▮▮▮▮▮▮▮▮▮▮
▮▮▮▮▮▮▮▮▮▮ *not sure anything else has a higher priority
than creating a link with that powerhouse of nature."*

*"You get this one only because my preferred resources are unavailable.
This is a discreet operation. My research oracle uncovered the
inception date and artifact information this morning. No one else
knows except for my researcher, myself, and now you. Not even the
President of International Affairs knows, much less the Board.*

*"If any of this leaves this office before that bid, I'll make it a personal
goal in FY '13 to castrate you with rusty nail clippers."*

*-Zachary Harrison, V.P. of International Affairs, Avalon Group.*

Ah, Mr. Harrison, you silver-tongued devil, you. I'll have to
remember a nice Solstice present for you, like a lump of coal...

"Hroayoauahnaoy!"

...aaaaaand that's when a rather agitated voice interrupts my
reverie. Well, the voice and the distinctive ring of a sword being drawn.
More arresting than the naked blade, however, are the eyes of the

swordsman. Haunted and bloodshot, the pale jade eyes seem torn between me and the surrounding forest.

Quickly assessing the young man, maybe 17, I begin to feel very uneasy. Not just haunted, he feels hunted. His staccato words accent ragged breathing as he slowly circles me in ripped and muddy clothing. His hair must have been bowl-cut at one point, but now it's shaggy, unkempt, and dances across his eyes. Yet the sword remains steady and upright in his calloused hands.

The sword... his sword... glinting in the morning sun. As he circles, the rich light brings out delicate scrollwork on the blade and certain details on the cross-guard. Most importantly, centered on the guard, is the etched dove with a crown of stars. The sword of Sophia. Well-well, I will never doubt the accuracy of the Avalon Group's brain trust again.

He hisses syllables. A question this time, I think. Need to keep him talking while I adjust. Although I know he's speaking English, it's 16th century English spoken by someone who looks equally prepared to gut me, climb a tree, or just fall over. It's like trying to read a newspaper in a funhouse mirror streaked with fingerprints.

Fortunately, I'm a quick study. In the time it takes to slowly raise my hands and stand, I have a young child's command of the language. After a few moments of weaving unsteadily, I adjust completely and am fluent. The only difficulty now is hearing each other over the rising wind.

I try a disarming smile, "Let's try this again at a civilized pace, now that world has stopped spinning. My name is Jackson... or, Jax, if you promise not to slice me open. You?"

His shoulders drop half an inch and, while not sheathing the sword, he stops circling me and switches from a two-handed grip to one. There's also an ounce less of the crazed tension in his eyes.

"My name is William, William Wythers, but I'm afraid that civilization will never again be my home or destination." He chuckles but the pitch starts to climb, threatening to devolve into a mad wail. But William coughs, clamps his teeth, and bows his head to bring himself back under control.

# TIMESLIP

Distracted, William continues, "I... I'm sorry for that. The thing that chases me hasn't let me come closer than shouting distance to anyone, native or colonist, for more than two months now. I pray every night for these demons to return to whatever green hell they come from... or to just finish my torment and..."

He pauses as a sound floats over the moaning wind; a two-tone call, like a bird, but deep in register. The hairs on my neck immediately stand on end and my body reflexively shifts into a crouch. William's response is less measured, if more effective.

He runs.

I follow.

A crackling boom erupts behind us and glancing back I see a forest nightmare with no right place in sun. A vast writhing mass of vegetation, easily fifty feet across, has swept onto our path and just obliterated a giant maple. Ropey yet decaying shapes of ivy, moss, bramble, and deadwood undulate and ripple in a sickly green wave. Crouching atop the wave, riding it, is a green figure blowing into a pan pipe. Each note evokes a different flavor of fear along my spine... and I can't control it. None of my training works.

I run. A puppet on the pipe's strings, I run like hell itself was upon us. Even so, I manage to stay close to William.

Moments stretch to minutes and branches whip our faces, earning me some free scratches. I try sprinting away from William several times but the verdant horror stays focused on him. I try peeling off and throwing things at it, but no reaction. Focusing my will, I plunge back to William's side after every experiment.

William stumbles several times. He's got to be running on the fumes of fumes but he rights himself every time and finds some new motivation to keep running. The willpower is almost frightening in its own right.

Curiously, the tidal mass behind us never catches up, but provides a persistent and menacing presence. William is absolutely being herded. And so am I, by extension. The salient questions are, of course, "where to", "by whom", and "why". But the pipes leave me no head for answers.

# TIMESLIP

Exhaustion claims William in the late afternoon and I whip around to protect him. But there's nothing there. The bloody thing evaporated. Between gasps, he explains the pattern. He runs, he collapses, he runs some more and then stops in the evening. This hunter never catches him. Never approaches at night. But it always returns in the morning and the dreadful pipe's fear sets him running anew.

So it was for him and so it becomes for us both.

Over the next hellish week, William tries to persuade me to leave. He tries all manner of rationale but I prove what I've proven before: I'm a huge pain in the ass. Finally, on the third night, I tell him why I'm here. In as plain an English as I can muster, I tell him everything; the future, the sword's past, my suspicions of his role. He cycles through the various stages of disbelief, anger, despair, angst, and back to anger. In the end, I ply his exhaustion and acceptance trumps incredulity. He even agrees to let me wield the Sword of Sophia if it comes to direct confrontation.

After the grand reveal, the flow of information improves. By the seventh night, I match William's recounting with my geography and I know where we're being herded. This morning we passed through the highway195/495 interchange just west of Cobalt City. We are less than 10 miles from the heart of Lafayette Park where there will be a statue commemorating General Lafayette atop a curiously colored outcropping of exposed bedrock.

Tomorrow's waxing moon will find us there and begin the end to my mission and William's long nightmare. Looking at William's face, haggard even in sleep, I struggle to make this task satisfying. Or acceptable. Or just plain bearable. In the end, I simply decide that I'm a bastard and let exhaustion take me where dreams never follow.

The next night we're exhausted again but the situation has definitely changed. We break through the forest into a clearing just a couple hours before sunset. In the heart of the clearing stands the bedrock outcropping, though it's jagged and a uniform tan color; very different from the 2012 version. More curiously, the pipe music fades the moment we set foot on the clearing's grass... along with the wind. Both are now scant murmurs with little effect.

We try darting out of the clearing in every direction but a wall of slumping forest blocks us every time. Unsurprised and defeated, we camp on the outcropping. William naps while I watch the stars come alive in the sky... waiting for the moon to arrive, redden and start the last chapter.

Two hours later I nudge William as the moon blushes with the first kiss of crimson from the perihelion eclipse. Screaming straight in from Cape Cod, the wind assaults our ears... and our noses. Ah gods, I hate fish.

No pipes, but to the north of us, I hear the groaning of trees; first swaying to the wind but then, with moist torturous sounds of uprooting, two ancient white oaks come shambling towards us. In the thunder of the ground beneath me, I feel **much** more empathy for Macbeth.

This is why the V.P. wanted someone else. I'm an excellent field agent but I do have my limitations. My gift is learning, highly accelerated learning. Thirty-seven languages paint my dreams, where I commit sciences, arts and philosophy to memory. Honestly, my genes almost proved the golden ticket into the finest psych ward in Paris. But the Avalon Group found me and taught me the tricks to handle my voracious mind.

But my body learns as well, insistently keeping up with my mind. A doctor once told me I had forced him to use a logarithmic scale to measure my mirror neurons. I learned the basics of Kung Fu when I was six years old after watching a Bruce Lee marathon. The 1992 Olympics were a revelation on the beauty of movement.

The Avalon Group didn't have to teach me how to use these skills, so much as how to keep them under control. Having a lover playfully slap your face is decidedly different than a mugger trying to pistol-whip you. But in that exquisite moment when time slows and all you can discern is speed and trajectory... well, the body doesn't always care about the finer details of intent.

As effective as this makes me in a host of situations, there are a number of tricks that I don't possess. I can't shoot flames from my fingers, nor deflect bullets. I'm much slower than a sprinting cheetah and true psychics scare the piss out of me. Animals have no special affinity for me and the closest I get to flying is leaping between Quayside buildings with my parkour group. I may be an elite human being but I can see why Harrison sought a more "super" operative.

But I'm the one who came and I'm the one that William is depending on to save his 16$^{th}$ century ass.

*Merde.*

"Jaaaaaaaaax..." William sounds slightly awed.

I whip around and follow his eyes. "You have **got** to be kidding me!"

In the depths of the forest, the reddening moon shows two treetops surging towards us amidst the canopy, like monstrous sharks greedy for blood. They tower over us a good eighty feet. They lance the heart of me with an awful humility. I've danced amidst hulking brutes and technological horrors but Nature's canvas is just so vast!

They stop at the clearing, maybe forty feet apart.

We remember to breathe.

"What's going on, Jax? I thought that the pipe player would be coming for me tonight, not a pair of... some... whatever these new abominations are!"

William's mind is about to break. He's got good reason, actually. I'm scared enough that my filters are slipping: I hear the Thoreau in me laugh giddily while Ansel Adams won't shut up about shifting angle for better composition. An overabundance of education really is off-putting in moments of abject crisis.

I breathe deeply, bring my filters back up, and use the ancient defense of fools everywhere: puns.

"Perhaps, William, we were meant to go *barking* mad or simply remain *stumped*. Or maybe these are *ashen*-faced apologists for the piper's ill-treatment of us. Clearly we should get to the *root* of the problem instead of simply *pining* for divine inspiration. Yes, indeed, I feel a need to *branch* out in my investigations beyond *needling* the unknown and *leafing* through possibilities. Clearly, *sapping* these stalwarts is a *knotty* endeavor but it would be a *crowning* achievement in tonight's *thorny* labors.

His shock turns to amazement...which turns to chuckling...and finally blossoms into full-throated laughter, bringing his mind back from a mad precipice. These beautiful and very human sounds also clean the wound of my own terror, allowing me to remember the Sword of Sophia.

"Ah ha!" I cry, drawing the sword from William's scabbard. "What say you, William? Shall I let the future history of this blade carry me to glory as the champion barrel-maker of this, or any other, age? They are White Oak after all and would make a legendary number of whiskey barrels!" William continues laughing as I strike heroic poses that threaten to sprain my lower back.

## *"I Think Not."*

It's amazing how a bass rumbling can sound so feminine. Maybe I'm just projecting... but it *is* familiar. Either way, I pause in my mouthy antics and look at the trees.

While I played the Shakespearean fool, the towering oaks had grown intertwined with vines, leaves, and all manner of arboreal detritus. Oh, and they started glowing a brilliant green. I really detest being upstaged but the formation of thirty-foot lips is really quite impressive.

Readying myself in a more functional stance, I find my mouth still foolish, "Welcome to the party, madame piper, we were beginning to feel positively stood up".

*"You stink of fear and stale dreams, little mortal. You will be so much more appealing with your skin in tatters and your last breath scattered on the winds."*

The trite prose clues me in. "For an immortal tour de force, you sound like an old playmate of mine. She had a taste for violent passions while her doggerel prose was violence on the ears.." Lifting the sword high, I press, "Did you come back for a little *edge*-play? I'm sure you'd find it inspirational... *Bocage*."

Leaves, twigs, and vines should never smile. Just never. That goes double for laughing. I'm all for mirth and merriment but not in a massive, malevolent, glowing mouth under a bloody moon.

Keeping my eyes on the mirthful vegetation, I call back to William, "Stay on the stones, watch our backs, and remember that in life, unlike chess, checkmate doesn't mean the game's over."

"Um, I thought you said 'while nothing's impossible, some things are highly improbable and need a great deal of luck'." William actually does a decent imitation of my lecturing voice.

"Well, yes, but I thought the abbreviated version would be far more heroic given the circumstances."

"Honestly, Jax, it only served to put me in mind of what to put on your gravestone."

"You know, William, I think I could go for a bit less honesty right now."

**"Oh I don't know, Jax. I think your bravado could stand a little honest inspection. In fact, let me help you with that right now."**

The mouth snaps open, revealing a malaise of colors, scents and sounds that are both nauseating and familiar. The redolence of maple, oak and sea salt are replaced by the sharp tang of ozone and... strawberries? As a white iris blossoms from the center of the mad tableau, the world around me slows to a crawl.

Oh good, one of my better tricks. Physical crisis provokes mental acuity and I need all I can get. As the iris spirals open I string together enough clues to realize what's happening. Mostly. However, the realization at whom I should be seeing in mere seconds kinda ruins all the comfort of my survival instincts kicking in.

Of course, it's Bocage, but that's much less important than her likely titles. Strawberries mean she's a time traveler and that sparks a logic cascade that's 90% subconscious, 99% reliable and 100% guaranteed to hurt. She's an agent of Avalon Group's upper management. In fact, given the manifested abilities with the flora, she has to be a Page to the Board and a Daughter of the Green Mother, herself.

If I survive, I'm SO asking for a raise.

The iris fully opens and transports in a bald, beautiful, and immensely imposing figure clothed in... is that phosphorescent algae? Huh, that's a new one. But ammunition is ammunition. In the tradition of knaves throughout the ages, I take what is given.

I fire my first salvo in French. "Really, Bocage? Algae? Is that what passes for haute couture in Paris these days?"

Bocage actually pauses. The gentle arc of her smile dampens but her left eyebrow stays elevated; irritated. Good.

"Careful, Jax. That mouth of yours has always been double-edged. There are many who would happily see your tongue garnishing my trophy collection." Ohhhhh-kay... Trophies... Yes, indeed, a very, very large raise.

Her first steps look oddly hesitant but the algae flows downward to thicken around her feet.

My smile grows a touch ironic, "Are you saying that there's a solution here that doesn't involve me becoming mulch?"

Fifty feet away, bathed in the ruddy, reflected sunlight, she laughs. "Oh no, not at all. I was implying that the more you talk, the more I'll enjoy playing with my food before I actually dine." Ah, this close I can see her sharpened teeth. Honestly, it's quite unfair to give me this much opportunity for fun.

Time for the second volley. I snap my fingers, "Of course! That sense of elan, your subtle charms, clearly you've picked your style from walking the streets *a la Place Pigalle?*" I chuckle low in my throat as her face contorts into an ugly caricature of amusement. Sadly, the best place for a gentleman is the bedroom, not the battlefield.

She launches with a howl that distorts the air between us. Claws extend from fingertips as algae flows up from her torso to thicken around her arms. She looks like a feral Mega Man and I can't help laughing genuinely.

Eyes fixed on Bocage's charge, I return to 16th century English and shout behind me, "William, stay behind the highest rock and don't you dare run." It's his best chance. Yes, I'm a bastard, but it turns out that even bastards find their limits.

I charge forward. Keeping my eyes on Bocage's center of mass I watch her limbs blur with speed and bloodlust. I give her the anticipated first clash, a quickly slashing at her knees. Her forearms readily counter with thickened algae armor but twists to then snatch at the blade.

Fortunately my mind races along as I learn her tactics, one muscle twitch at a time. This first engagement seems to take minutes, not seconds, and allows my reflexes to compensate for her raw speed... at least in part.

Bocage's claws scrape down the length of the blade as I draw it back and roll further backwards with the motion. She lunges and I let my instincts lead in our dance around the base of the outcropping. I flick small slashes at her wrists and ankles while occasionally swiping stronger strokes at the thinner algae along her stomach. She lets the strikes land on her extremities but dances away from well-aimed blows at her middle. Sadly, the sword does nothing to her algal armor. *Merde!*

All the while, I dance, letting the wellsprings of aikido and capoeira flow, keeping my skin intact. Still, Bocage's smile says she's holding back. When a desperate dive has me roll up with a clear view of the mammoth oaks, my mind distractedly notes that the portal is still open. She scores a deep rake down my left arm, which immediately begins to itch.

A throaty laugh vibrates from her as she pulls back to taste my vintage on her claws. "You *are* a nimble little minx, I'll give you that, Jax. But I've drawn first blood. I can taste your desperation. Soon my infection will steal your strength and deliver you to the earth. Concede now and I'll let you pass on as a human."

# TIMESLIP

Under the ruddy eclipse I see, even now, small dark buds forming around the edges of the wound. My stomach turns but I push it down, along with the terror.

*<Crack!>*

Bocage stumbles forward, head down. Over her shoulder I see William pick up another rock, ready to throw. Oh William, you shouldn't have...

Bocage's legs bunch for a leap as I rush forward to tackle her. She looks up and our eyes meet for half a heartbeat to paint her joyfully malicious plans for William. In mid-lunge, one of the buds on my wound erupts in a puff of thick yellow pollen. The pain is so surprising and intense that the sword drops from my hand in a paroxysm of agony. Gracefully turning her leap at William into an exaggerated forward flip, Bocage reverses direction and snatches up the fallen blade.

My scream of pain and anguish blends with her exultant howl, even as William's second throw finds its mark. Through my own haze I see a dark trail run down Bocage's hip. Okay, I take it back. William, you're a genius. Hopefully the endorphins will prevent her from realizing that she's bleeding.

I finally set aside the pain in my arm and follow as she leaps up the outcropping, sword in hand. Bounding along, I almost slip on my second leap, a full second behind the springing Death headed for William. Cursing, I notice that I was nearly undone by a glob of algae. I keep my hope banked deep inside me but I let a plan begin to form.

William scrambles along the top of the stones but finds no more stones. Bocage flings herself along the ground instead of leaping high and catches William off guard. The trip turns into a pin as the Green Daughter rolls onto her prey and digs her free claws into William's shoulder. His face contorts in a horrible mask of transcending pain. Something twists deep inside of me and I can't accept my failure even as it burns into my memory.

Bocage releases William's shoulder and raises the sword high, letting the moon paint a picture of the blade's future; a study in scarlet. She smiles in triumph. The sword starts to descend.

My mind accelerates further and the world turns to tar.

The blade is a streak of blood as I make my last futile charge. In the gruesome tableau of William's final moments I focus on his face. I owe him that much. But instead of finding his gaze locked on the descending blade, Bocage, or even myself, William stares at a point just in front of me on the ground.

A nine-inch shard of stone. Oh...sweet William... I could kiss you.

I let hope explode in my heart, driving out the nuisances of pain and despair. Cycling through my filters, I coax my muscles to catch up with my mind. Quite obligingly, even as the sword is a quarter-way through its arc, I feel the switch to an old set of skills first learned on broken pavement when I was eight. Called the most egalitarian sport in the world, football skills are eminently portable. Even into 16th century New England.

The angle is all wrong to aim for Bocage's head so I aim lower.

My left foot plants solidly, I stop thinking, and I put all my fury, all my guilt, and all my hope into the swing of my right foot.

Time realigns amongst the players in this fateful game as blood paints the stone above William's head.

Bocage's blood.

William's face erupts in a disbelieving smile to match the wretched cry as Bocage tumbles. The stone skewers her right hand and though she's standing I can see that shock has hit surprisingly hard. I also see algae receding from her hand and then wrist. Nor does it stop at her shoulder or even her stomach.

Bocage also notices the odd behavior of her organic armor. She splits her attention between the movement on her body and staggering away from William. I interpose myself, dropping into a defensive crouch. Even wounded, her full speed and strength are terrible. The burst pod has released small tendrils that continue to crawl across my arm, heading for my shoulders and chest.

# TIMESLIP

However, William surprises me again, even as I prep for another charge from one of the reputedly indefatigable Daughter of the Green Mother. A guttural cry tears from William as something snaps and he raggedly sprints past me, sword in hand.

Scorn somehow sneaks past her grimace as Bocage ducks under William's wild swing and knocks the sword out of his hands. Or at least, I'm pretty sure that's what she meant to do. Despite my shock, I'm probably the least surprised of us as a pod from William's wounded shoulder erupts, causing his swing to spasm wildly.

Bocage's block is out of place and she instinctively follows up with her bad hand. The impromptu change puts her body out of position and they collide. Out of control, they tumble to the edge of the outcropping and fall out of sight. Heart in my throat, I lunge for William's feet but only skid to the edge.

The wind explodes from me and it takes far longer than I want for my vision to clear. I listen... but all my ears tell me is that my breathing is still ragged, the wind is calming, and the crazy soundscape of the portal is still in full force. Everything else is silent.

In a few measured heartbeats, my vision clears to add a richness to my speculations that I neither want nor will ever forget.

The drop-off was very steep and had a cluster of small spires at the base. Though Bocage led the fall, in those last moments, she spun William beneath her. But William hadn't given up; with one hand on the sword he'd used his wounded arm to clasp Bocage to him.

They both ran out of time and were impaled on several spires of rock. Lying outstretched, both hands still clasped to the sword even as blood sheathed their skins and the stone underneath.

As I scramble down, cradling my increasingly burning shoulder, I see that Bocage's face is set forever in a furious glare. Through my tears, William's face is carved into a determined smile. I stumble back and sat down on the grass, trying to just focus on breathing, and ignore the race between the moon's face and William's.

I stay in the clearing until sunrise. Already in a masochistic mood, I meticulously apply one of the stones William had thrown to scrape my wound clear of Bocage's infection. Lucky me, it works. My fortune also seems determined to have me try for that raise, too, as the portal stays open throughout my moody vigil.

When the sun crests the horizon, I receive the last piece of mission data. The remaining algae along Bocage's skin go mad with activity once the sun strikes. Even the remains on the outcropping ripple and erupt, increasing in volume hundreds, even thousands, of times.

The algae's frenzy is greatest where it mingles with blood... a viridian cathedral rising from the spent life of plant and animal. The creeping architecture envelops the cooled bodies and the sun-warmed blade between them. Where the algae touches stone, the green material sizzles and then fuses in angry susurrations even as the top layers surge still higher.

In a few short minutes, the algal growth covers the sides of the outcropping. What's more, it smoothes to leave an almost uniform pillar of stone and crystallized algae; tan at the bottom, emerald topped, and striated along the sides. An ideal base for Lafayette's statue to acquire pigeon droppings in 2012.

The transformation complete and seemingly solid, I stand up and turn away from William's grave. Assuming I survive the debriefing I think I'll take some time off and pay a proper visit to the memorial at Lafayette Park... but, first things first.

Bracing myself for the nausea, I step into the portal and fervently hope that my V.P.'s shoes are in range of my stomach on the other side.

**S. Aarron Kemp.** *After three and a half decades, Aarron has finally learned that fire is hot, coffee can bite, and that his feet are magnets for broken glass. A native Seattle product, he's finally given in to his loudest voices and written a finished story. Now, heady with power, he sets his eyes on the ever-elusive tasty gluten-free croissant.*

# TIMESLIP

War at Home
1976

Cole Washington stepped off the bus at Mason Station in downtown Cobalt and was hit by a gob of spit on his cheek and a murmur of "Baby killer." In two tours in the 'Nam, he was confident that he had killed no babies. He had come to expect the resentment, and he bore up under the stares and name-calling with the same even temper that got him through the war. He dug a napkin from the pocket of his dress greens and wiped the spittle from his scarred, dark cheek. Cole hadn't planned on returning to Cobalt City as a hero, at least not since he re-upped, but to return as a pariah hadn't been on the agenda either.

With a world-weary sigh, Cole hoisted his canvas duffel over his shoulder. He had arranged to meet with his father out front, but a quick survey of the cars turned up no sign of the promised '64 Buick Skylark. It was getting on towards 10pm, and the other two passengers had already vanished into the night.

A kid, no more than sixteen or so, approached Cole from across the street wearing a thin, gray windbreaker to ward off the nighttime chill. His hands were thrust deep into the grubby pockets. He got close -- closer than Cole was comfortable with. He smelled like stale sweat. "You got a cigarette?"

Cole considered the pack of Camels in his jacket. "Fresh out."

There was a muted click as the kid flicked open a lock-blade knife. Cole hadn't even seen the kid take his hand from the pocket. "How about your wallet? Think you can find that, man?"

Sparks fired in Cole's eyes, lighting the close air between them an electric blue. "You want to rethink that?"

The would-be mugger was halfway across the street at a dead sprint before his knife hit the ground. Cole kicked it into the gutter. Damned if he wanted to see another knife after what happened to Judy. He wondered, as the kid vanished into the night, if the world was so small that this was the person who had also killed his wife. He quickly dismissed the thought. That was five years ago, and Judy's assailant had been an adult.

Wheels crunched on rotting asphalt as the familiar profile of his dad's car rounded the corner. Cole waved it down, though it was coasting into the curb as soon as he lifted his hand. Errol Washington cursed through the open passenger window. "I can see you standing there, boy. I ain't going blind quite yet."

Cole tilted the seat forward to toss his bag in the backseat. "It's been a few years, pops. I figured you might not recognize me."

Errol had packed a lot of living into his fifty-some years, and it was starting to show in his tightly trimmed hair and mustache gone mostly to gray. He rolled his head on a powerful neck in disbelief. "What kind of father don't recognize his own boy? Let me get you home and get some food in you. Prolly ain't had a real meal since you left Kentucky, have you?"

"No, sir."

With Cole secure in the car, his father pulled out into traffic, clicking his tongue. "I figured as much. Without the army telling you when to eat, sleep, and go to the bathroom, you're going to fall apart on me. Well, no worries. I put in a lasagna before I come to fetch you. John is there to take it out of the oven if we don't get back before the timer dings."

They caught up some on the trip from downtown to the old neighborhood. The tires hummed crossing the metal grill bridge to West Quayside, or West Key as the old-timers called it. Neon from the waterside casinos burned the night sky -- the Forbidden Palace, Bailey's Lucky Irish, the Golden Monkey each blazing as brightly as when Cole had shipped out. Once off the bridge, they lost the casino lights in the maze of small factories, storefronts, and isolated blocks of houses and apartment buildings. More store windows were boarded up than Cole had expected from his father's last letter. "Going out of business" and "Fire sale" signs decorated now-shuttered shops, and more than one lump shifted in a doorway as they passed. The only signs of life traveled in packs – young lions moving from one watering hole to another in search of a meal.

"What the hell happened here, pops?"

They approached a brightly lit building, the blazing lights marking it from two blocks away. Errol slowed the car as they got closer. "*That* happened," he said, not bothering to hide the contempt in his voice. Cars filled the street parking and the lot next door. A crowd was gathered on the sidewalk out front, dressed in short skirts, wide-lapels, platform shoes, and sunglasses even at night. There was enough polyester to build an ugly, colorful circus tent, enough hair spray to burn down a village. The sign above the door was chrome and neon in a rainbow of colors six feet high reading "Bifrost." A chill went down Cole's spine.

Cole whistled low, amazed by the visible opulence in an otherwise stagnating neighborhood. "A nightclub?"

"A disco," Errol said, almost choking on the word. "A *roller* disco. And what the hell kind of name is Bifrost?"

"It's the name of the rainbow bridge into Valhalla, realm of the Norse gods," Cole said without thinking.

His father was quiet for some time, processing the information. "That what they're teaching kids in school these days? Norse myth?"

"I learned that from a friend in the army," Cole said quietly, only half lying. "Johnson used to talk about it all the time."

But Johnson never told him about Bifrost. The laid-back surfer turned soldier knew mythology pretty well, perhaps too well. He talked at great length to Cole about the Norse gods and their place in the world. They had been lazy, informal stories, like ones Cole told about the diner or the friends back home. But Johnson had never mentioned the rainbow bridge. That knowledge had come from very hard-to-get books that Cole had bartered for. They were needed to help explain what happened when Johnson's body was taken away that day on the hill.

Cole was shell-shocked, stunned by the NVA mortars raining down on their position for two straight weeks. Every night, when the mortars fell among their position, lightning crashed behind the enemy lines. It scared the hell out of the other men in Cole's unit, though they were glad for some kind of air support. They didn't know why the lighting was only hungry for VC blood – only Johnson and Cole knew the truth of that. Over the years, the lightning saved their asses more than once in tough situations, and Cole was no dummy. One final night, as explosions rocked the ground, and the air filled with the sound of burning dirt and ozone, Cole was close enough to see the sparks in Lars Johnson's eyes.

It wasn't long – just a few seconds. But it was enough to prove that Johnson hadn't been entirely full of shit. And it helped explain what happened later.

That night, Cole watched his friend die, blown in half by a lucky mortar strike. His world froze in an instant, the boom and whoosh a distant echo. Through the smoke and the light of fires and the biggest lightning storm since creation, Cole watched a lone helicopter descend. A woman with braids and spear reached out. Johnson stood and joined her. He spared one last look over his shoulder at Cole, during which understanding and so much more passed between them. Only as the helicopter lifted off, time and noise returning to the hellish din, did Cole Washington notice that the helicopter was painted with the name Valkyrie.

The car bumped up onto the twin lines of concrete pavers along the side of the house and snapped Cole out of his memory. He climbed out, and after fetching his bag, followed his father inside.

The house smelled of smoke when they opened the door. Errol waded through to the kitchen, cursing under his breath. "Damn lasagna burned. Should have come out of the oven half an hour ago. Samson was supposed to be here taking care of this!"

"Maybe he fell asleep," Cole answered. He looked out the window to John Samson's house across the street. The lights were on, and a crack of light showed through a door left ajar. Two shapes moved in silhouette against the blinds. "I'm going to go check on him, pops. You okay to deal with the dinner?"

"I'll be fine. I might be able to save some of it," Errol called from the other room. "But don't bother bringing that darned fool over for dinner. His fault for falling asleep on the job."

Airborne Rangers training took over when Cole hit the street. He moved fast, shadow to shadow, approaching the house. His eyes did not stray from the dark shapes in the window. The distinctive grunts and thuds of a beating reached his ears by the time his feet found the steps of the porch.

Sparks jumped to Cole's eyes. He clenched and unclenched his hands and thunder rolled ominously in the distance. Cole straightened, but deep in his heart, he knew he really wasn't entirely Cole Washington anymore. The avatar of Thor rode his shoulders like a well-worn coat, passed from friend to friend, soldier to soldier in the heat of battle as the All-Father intended. The porch creaked beneath his step and the sound of fighting inside came to an abrupt stop.

Cole gave in to instinct. Two swift steps carried him to and kicked open the door, revealing two punks standing over the prone, broken body of an old man. The skinny black kid held a steak knife, blade glistening wetly. The Latino punk had an axe handle in his meaty fists, brow beaded with exertion.

The knife waved in his direction, only vaguely threatening. "This ain't none of your business, brother."

"You gonna back up off my friend, there?" Cole said. He could see the uncertainty in their faces. It was something he was used to seeing when he channeled the thunder god. Other than the sparks, there was nothing to indicate that he was anything other than just another Vietnam vet. But there was a presence, a weight, that Cole hadn't possessed before. Even though the two robbers couldn't see a difference, their lizard brain could feel it. This town had its share of super-heroes. The fact that Cole wasn't in some kind of costume didn't mean a damn thing.

The attackers hesitated, looked at each other. The Latino kid licked his lips nervously.

They made no effort to move.

Cole shrugged. Thunder inside the room. "You had your chance." He snapped his fingers and sent lightning bolts arcing to the attackers. The shock sent the two men flying across the sofa. He listened and heard both men moaning. They would live, but wouldn't be waking up for a while.

A third moan caught his ears – Mr. Samson. Cole knelt next to his father's long-time friend. He had been stabbed, but only once, in the arm. The wound looked clean. There was a raspy quality to the shallow breathing, which might be broken ribs or his lifetime of smoking. "Mr. Samson? Can you hear me?"

The old man rolled over and squinted up through a swollen eye. "Cole? Is that you, boy? What the hell happened?"

"You got your ass kicked, old man," Cole said. "But I'm here now. You okay to walk across the street and call the police?"

Mr. Samson thought it over, a brief self-assessment of what felt broken. He nodded. "Help me up and fetch my cane from next to that chair. But there's no way the cops are going to come to West Key for a robbery this time of night."

Cole helped the old man up. "Tell Cobalt City's boys in blue that the two robbers will be gift-wrapped for them." He stepped towards the fallen robbers. He could feel Thor itching to be let off the chain again. "But tell them to hurry."

Once he was alone with the two assailants, he let the god of thunder share his body again. Electricity arced through his sinews and gave him strength. Sparks turned his eyes to blue fireworks. His every move was a low, threatening rumble. He looked over the two men and chose the skinny black one to deal with first. Hairs stood out on the back of his hand as Cole reached out and touched his captive. Panicked, bloodshot eyes blinked open.

"You and me, we're going to talk." Cole rumbled. "Why you gotta hassle an old man in his own home?"

"Tino saw him paying for groceries this morning, and saw how much money he had in his wallet."

It had the ring of truth. John Samson had a pension from his long career at the bank. The check would have come in recently, and having spent so long in a bank, John didn't trust them with his money. The thin, beaten punk had track marks on the inside of his elbow, but none of them looked very recent. A touch of white powder lined the inside of his left nostril. Cocaine. Not a cheap fix, and a big step up from the horse he had been on until recently. The newly acquired taste was not an easy one to sustain. "You should quit the hard stuff, bro. It's an expensive habit."

"I don't know what you're talking about."

There had been drugs in West Key for a while. It wasn't the worst neighborhood in Cobalt City - that distinction went to the Hollow on the other side of the bridge. But the mix of warehousing, light industry, and residential this close to the legalized gambling of Quayside drew vices to be fed. But coke was a rich man's game, and this was not a rich part of town. Pot, pills, heroin, even angel dust were big business, yes. But not cocaine.

His thoughts turned to the Bifrost. It's what's wrong in West Key, according to his father. The name could have been a coincidence. "I'm only going to ask once, mother-fucker. Where do you get your fix?" Electricity jumped across his bared knuckles, his voice held the promise of a coming storm.

"The disco," the junkie said. "We get them at the roller disco."

"Who is your dealer?"

"He calls himself Loki. He's always there," the junkie said, real fear permeating his voice. "I think he's the owner."

Cole smiled. It was an expression entirely devoid of warmth. "How about you describe him to me? You do a good job, you'll still be awake when the cops get here."

Three minutes late, Cole Washington crossed the street, axe handle in his hand, image of a skinny white dude with a sloppy blonde afro and rainbow suspenders in his mind's eye. The junkie and his friend had been tied up with their own shoelaces - thumbs tied together, hands secured behind the back to the ankles. They wouldn't be going anywhere, even if the cops stopped at Sprinklehaus Donuts before showing up.

Cole stashed the axe handle behind the azaleas along the front porch. When he looked up, he spotted his dad's shadow falling across the screen door. "How is Mr. Samson doing, pops?"

Errol shuffled through the door with a cautious look over his shoulder. "He's been roughed up pretty bad, but he's had worse. Ambulance is on the way. He's making short work out of a creamsicle in the kitchen while we wait for the sirens."

"A couple of junkies did this," Cole said calmly. He watched his father's reaction carefully and saw no surprise. "That happen a lot these days?"

Errol pursed his lips, refusing to meet his son's eyes.

"That happen to you?" He knew the answer. His dad was a good-sized man, a hard worker all his life. But he was also getting older. There was a day when Cole knew his dad could take any other father on the block, should it come to that. That day was a long time ago.

"They got me twice," Errol said after a long pause. His voice was quiet, a strange cocktail of defiance just on the edge of trembling. "Not the same folks, based on what Samson told me, but there were two of them each time. First time, I fought back, even broke the nose on the first little bastard. Then they broke my arm in two places. Knocked me down, put it up over the curb and jumped on it. They told me I got off lucky. Broke my motherfucking arm and told me I was lucky. The next time I got mugged, they asked for my wallet and I didn't even look up."

Cole stepped onto the porch and squeezed his father's shoulder. It was enough to open up the tear ducts on both men, though Errol was by far the more emotional. "How come you didn't tell me that? You wrote me twice a week, and I had no idea."

"Didn't want you to be ashamed of your old man," Errol said. He sniffed, followed by a soft laugh. "Anyway, what my baby boy going to do – leave the Army and come fight the enemy in West Key?"

"Yeah, pops," Cole said. "Something like that." He turned his gaze out towards the Bifrost. He could make out the spotlight beams from the porch. Didn't look more than two clicks away. "You wait here with Mr. Samson. I'm going to go change out of my dress greens. Then I got a little errand to run in the neighborhood."

# TIMESLIP

Errol Washington looked up at his son, confusion giving way to a grim understanding. "You do what you feel you got to do. Anything you need from me?"

Cole shook his head, took half-a-step towards the door, turned back. "Actually, you remember that old leather coat of yours you said I could have? That still around?"

"I'll fetch it out of the closet for you now."

Cole smiled, an idea slowly taking shape. "Right on."

Barry White was singing the fuck out of "You're the First, the Last, My Everything," when Cole stepped through the double door of Bifrost. It was late, close to last call at any West Key bar. There were still dozens of people on the skate floor. He adjusted the collar and cuffs of his cocoa-colored leather car coat. The suppleness of the leather was enough to offset the stiffness in his back where the hidden axe handle rested against his spine. There was a full bar down the left side of the disco, the skate rental and curvy, orange chairs along the right. At the far end of the skate floor, a DJ booth towered like an altar to the gods of disco.

Hell... the music hadn't been around for more than a few years. Both Cole and the avatar that rode him knew whom the altar really serviced. He was there, rolling smoothly across polished hardwood. He was just as the junkie had described - bouncing blond 'fro, rose-tinted sunglasses, rainbow suspenders over a tight, sparkly blue top.

Loki, the God of Lies. From a hundred feet away, Thor and Loki could sense each other. Eyes locked across the distance. Thunder rolled. Raucous laughter sounded from the bar. Barry White gave way to The Hues Corporation. *So I like to know if you got the notion. Said, I'd like to know if you got the notion to rock the boat. Don't rock the boat, baby.*

Bouncers materialized, shadow-like at the veteran's side. He sensed them as much as saw them, their presence triggering survival instincts honed by years "in country." Thor sensed something as well - the smell of rock moss and raw meat. They were big - bigger than Cole, with the aura of avatars that lent extra gravity to their presence. Thor thought the word "Trolls" and Cole heard it loud and clear. It was comforting, in a way, to know that Loki intended to resort to violence at some point. It let Cole know that he hadn't overestimated the threat shining in the Key.

While the other skaters rolled on, oblivious to the confrontation, Loki rolled to a stop in the center of the rink, watching and waiting.

The bouncer on Cole's left got to show his hand first. "The boss says we can't have your kind in here. I'm going to have to ask you to leave."

Cole turned to face the bouncer, one eyebrow arched above a socket of blazing blue sparks. "And what kind does he think I am?"

Bouncer Two decided to get involved. "You here to skate, drink, or make some other kind of cash transaction?"

Cole decided not to dignify the second bouncer with his attention, but he did answer. "No."

The first bouncer smiled. He had jutting lower incisors. "That would be the kind we don't want. Unless there's something else we can do for you?" He cracked his knuckles.

"I'm here to ask you to close down Bifrost and get out of Cobalt City."

The two bouncers looked at each other, confused for a moment. This was not the answer they expected, apparently. Cole took the opportunity to work the axe handle free from the back of his belt. He thanked the spotty lighting in the disco for making his life easier as he let the weight of the wood slide through his hand along the back of his leg. The bouncers looked to their boss for some kind of guidance. The slender skater squared his shoulders, his posture no longer so playful as before. Though no words were exchanged, the meaning was clear.

The first bouncer put a meaty hand on Cole's shoulder. The contact helped Cole see his target clearly for the first time. There was a second shape there occupying the same space, something less than human, and easily two feet taller. "I'm going to enjoy snapping you into bite-sized pieces. How about we take this dance outside?"

Cole dropped back a step and thunder rolled in the distance, barely audible between the beats in the music. He led the two troll bouncers around to face him, taking another swift step back to find the perfect distance. Lightning flowed from an immeasurable space between his soul and the avatar of Thor. Dancing blue sparks ran down his arm, down the length of wood, and formed a mythically large hammer at the end.

As the two bouncers took a second to consider this new development, Cole swung with both hands on the haft. The blue, sparking hammer passed inches above the heads of the two bouncers. The two troll avatars that rode them, however, were not as lucky. The lightning severed them from their hosts, dispelling them back into the pool of myth.

The bouncers fell, unconscious without being touched.

Chaos erupted, but it was a city kind of chaos full of noise and flash with no real danger. Both men at the heart of the storm remained planted, stones in a stream as shouting bodies raced around them, heading towards exits. Only the most loyal of employees stayed behind with the two men, eight inhuman avatars lurking above and within human hosts.

Lightning coursed through Cole's sinews. Thunder roared in his heartbeat. "I'm trouble you don't want, man. Pack up and move out."

Strobe lights switched on, and when Loki rolled forward, he moved in broken, jittery frames. No, Cole realized, it wasn't just the one of him. With each flicker, the slender trickster split – first one, then two, then four, then eight, then sixteen, then thirty-two. A small army of Lokis crowded the front of the skate area, closing on Cole. "You aren't the Thor I remember," Loki said. "What happened to that scared surfer boy who got called off to fight for flag and freedom?"

"He got called home," Cole said. He tried to focus on the voice, to determine where it was coming from. With all the background sound, it was impossible. "You want Johnson, head off to Valhalla to look for him. But he sent Thor back with me."

"Aren't you a little black to be Thor?"

Cole smiled. "There you are, making this a race thing. Thor appreciates all those pure blood types keeping it real, but he cares more about strength of character. I don't expect you to understand that. And for the record, he's Thor, I'm not. And together, we're someone else, you dig?"

The swarm of Loki surrounded him, the voice coming from everywhere and nowhere at once. "What do you suggest I call you, then?"

"You can use the same name your mama used last night," Cole said, tightening his grip on the hammer. "Call me Midnight Thunder!"

The newly christened hero dropped to one knee, slamming the butt of his weapon to the floor. Lightning arced in an electrical storm worthy of a god. Bolts slammed through a few of the Lokis advancing towards him, blackening the polished wood of the rink. Other bolts forked out, striking the advancing army of guardian avatars. Several staggered, some fell. A second wave of lightning cascaded from his hammer, disrupting a few more Lokis and dropping the last of the other warriors.

The lights continued to flicker and strobe in defiance of all the electricity flying about. In the darkness between flashes, glimpses of twisted, dark hells, feasting halls, bloodstained fields of ice, and crystal lakes surrounded by mountain peaks assailed his vision. Through it all, Loki advanced, his number growing to replace those that the lighting had disrupted.

He felt a sting in his side, the bite of a thin silver blade hurled from the darkness. Then another. Painful, yes, but not debilitating. Lightning surged through his blood, burning out any possible toxins, healing the wounds. With a roar, Midnight Thunder went into a spin, the hammer held wide. The arc of the hammer's head passed through Loki after Loki, dispelling them. Fake. All fake.

Loki's resonant laughter filled the Bifrost. "What are you going to do? Smash this place up with your hammer? You'll be in jail in a day. The papers will paint you as a villain, a lunatic, another unhinged Vietnam vet. Is that what you want?"

The thought cut deep into Cole's deepest fears. What was he? Even when he was channeling Thor, he was a soldier - nothing more and nothing less. Loki embodied mischief and trickery. It didn't take a genius to see how quickly public sentiment would turn against the

Midnight Thunder. And once the news got out about his war record, it would smear all veterans. He couldn't do that. Not to his brothers.

He tossed the axe handle out into the middle of the skate floor, the lightning head now gone. "I'll do better than that, Loki. I'll take you and your operation apart piece by piece. You might be a god, but you need to get your drug supply from somewhere, and you need customers. You go ahead and keep Bifrost open, but trust me on this man. You're in for one hell of a war. You dig?"

No one stopped Cole on the way out. Thor had gone back to sleep by the time he was a block away. It was another full block before he realized that someone was walking next to him – had been walking next to him for a while. This man wore a black, hooded cloak, the hood barely concealing albino-white hair. Despite the strange appearance, Cole didn't feel threatened. If this had been someone wanting to hurt him, he would have done it already.

"How long have you been following me?" he asked without breaking stride back towards his father's home.

The answer came from a deep, echoing place, like it was from the end of a long, stone hallway. "Long enough. I have had my own interactions with the gods, though mine were Egyptian rather than Nordic. I felt it best to observe for a while first."

"What kind of interactions?"

The stranger laughed hollowly. "I angered two of them, and was cursed. I've spent a long time trying to set it straight."

"How long?"

"About 3,000 years. Now, about this war of yours..."

Cole cocked an eyebrow. He felt Thor resurface, get his bearings, then fade away satisfied. "It's going to get ugly. You sure you can want in?"

"I'm a 3,000 year old sorcerer who has extensive experience with vengeful gods. I'll manage."

Cole laughed. "I think we'll get along just fine. Welcome to the war."

# TIMESLIP

**Nathan Crowder.** *The eldest child of an existentialist librarian and a teacher/child-care specialist, Nathan had always tended towards the literary. Now living in the Bohemian wilds of Seattle's Greenwood neighborhood, he plies his trade writing super-hero novels for the Cobalt City universe, as well as fiction both short and long for anthologies and online publications, having been selected for two best-of collections in the past year. Not content to live within genre bounds, he is nevertheless a member of the HWA, and has his sights set on other affiliations in the future.*

# TIMESLIP

## Daddy's Little Girl
### 1890

At the door to the study, Eleanor Castille paused for a moment. She dropped her long skirt back into place and ran her hands over her hair, trying to mask the fact that she had been running. She calmed her breathing and reached for the door.

Off to the side, she heard someone clear his throat. She glanced over, ready to admonish her little brother, Edmond, that he should be in bed. The young man to the left of the door was not five-year-old Edmond, but rather someone about her own age. Recognition dawned as she realized that the man was the son of the new doctor. Eleanor tried to remember his name, but found herself at a loss. Something beginning with a B, she thought.

She exchanged quick pleasantries, consciously using formal address to skirt her lapse in memory. He followed her lead, and then they looked at each other awkwardly for a few long moments. Finally, Eleanor spoke again. "I must see my father."

Hiram Castille was surrounded by household servants and the doctor, a regular visitor to the Castille household since his arrival in Cobalt City last winter. The servants moved aside as Eleanor approached, but the doctor remained by her father's side, tying a bandage on his left forearm. Eleanor pressed her eyes tightly shut at the sight of the crimson stain that already bloomed on the wrapping there. Regardless of the cause, a forearm injury was a serious one for her father.

While most of the world knew Hiram as simply an upstanding Cobalt City businessman and benefactor to the city, he frequently used the cover of darkness to take on the persona of his alter ego, the Huntsman. Armed with a bow, he ensured that the streets of Cobalt City were safe for its citizens.

"Eleanor," he said in a thin, quiet voice, much different from his usual confident tone.

"Yes, Father, I'm here. What happened?"

Hiram glanced at the doctor. "Doctor Mathias, will you leave us for a moment?"

"Sir? Your wounds are... substantial."

"I understand that, Doctor. I need to have a private word with my daughter. She is the lady of the house, after all. She needs to be informed of what is to be done."

Doctor Mathias stiffened, but nodded. "Very well, sir. I shall await her word before I return." He bowed formally, which Eleanor had barely enough presence of mind to acknowledge with a curtsy, and left the room.

Eleanor moved immediately to her father's side, and knelt beside the couch. "Father, what happened?"

"Some sort of mechanical creations, fashioned to look like our former presidents. They're guarding a warehouse in Quayside, near the meatpacking district. I couldn't get close enough to see much more than that. They're well armed automatons, Eleanor. Far more resilient than others I've seen. Far too well armed to just be a normal security detail."

"What shall I do, then?"

"Victor is collecting a few samples of what their weapons did to our carriage, and you should take those, along with what I just told you, to your Uncle Louis."

"But Father, Uncle Louis has not had the full training! I have more training than he does!" Eleanor exclaimed.

"Yes, Eleanor. But if God sees fit to take me, and if Louis were to fail in this attempt, that makes you the only remaining Castille able to teach your brother what he needs to know to take up the mantle of the Huntsman."

Eleanor rose from her father's side and turned to stare out the window. "It's because I'm a girl, isn't it?"

Hiram did not answer immediately. Eleanor sighed inwardly, certain that her father would respond with some answer that made it seem that her safety was his primary concern. "Eleanor, you are my only daughter. I cannot send you out to finish what I was not able to do.

Louis is prepared for such an eventuality." Hiram's voice broke with a sob. "I could never forgive myself if I lost you."

"If Edmond were 17, you would not hesitate to send him in your stead." She clapped her hand to her mouth as soon as she had spoken, shocked that she had voiced herself so forcefully.

Hiram sighed. "Perhaps you are right, Eleanor. However, that does not change my opinion. Louis will take care of this."

Eleanor composed her face carefully, and sat on the edge of the couch. She leaned forward and smoothed her father's hair. "As you wish, Father. You said the carriage was damaged in the attack?"

"Not severely damaged. Nothing that Victor won't have fixed by morning."

"I can ride to Uncle Louis's house before morning. I will take your equipment with me, and then he can begin work as soon as he arrives in Cobalt City. We'll have this taken care of before the doctor allows you to get out of bed."

"That's my girl," Hiram said, patting his daughter's arm gently. A grimace of pain slid across his face, and Eleanor rose.

"Doctor Mathias? My father needs you now." The door to the study opened immediately, as though the doctor had been waiting directly outside the entire time. Eleanor gave a quick curtsy and hurried into the hallway. The doctor's son was no longer waiting, but he had left a book in the chair he formerly occupied. She picked up the book idly, noting that it was one of the war treatises from her father's library. Her maid stood nearby, and Eleanor handed her the book. "Olivia, I need my riding habit ready in ten minutes and my horse in twenty. It appears I have a job to do."

Eleanor padded softly across the warehouse rooftop. In her left hand, she carried her father's bow. With her right, she clutched at the edges of her cloak, pulled tight to her body to help muffle the sound of the chain mail shirt she wore. The armor was too large for her, meant to fit her father's broad chest, but was surprisingly lightweight. Her eyes darted amongst the shadows on the rooftop, looking for any sign of movement other than her own. A strong wind rattled empty bottles and cans across the rough tarred surface, and wafted foul odors from the meatpacking district and nearby warehouses. Eleanor remained still until the wind died down, trying to breathe through the edge of her hood to minimize the stench.

As she waited, she spotted a door on the rooftop. She moved slowly to the entrance and jiggled the doorknob. Finding it locked, she set to work with a hairpin as her father had taught her. The cylinders clicked into place, and Eleanor opened the door, which spilled a sliver of golden light across the rooftop. Eleanor froze, bowing her head slightly to keep her face obscured by the hood of the cloak, to ensure that her entrance was not noticed. After what seemed like more than a minute, she slipped through the doorway.

Inside the building, Eleanor moved more quickly. She tiptoed down a flight of well-lit stairs, seeking the shadows. She found them on a fragile-looking catwalk of steel and wood, suspended high above the floor of the warehouse.

From her vantage point, the details of the work were not immediately apparent. She could see large bubbling vats that emanated an acrid stench, bathed in the glow of electrical lights. Two long worktables spanned the length of the warehouse. Each of these held metal parts, which workers were assembling into oversized rifles, far larger than a normal man could wield.

Around the perimeter of the workspace, a group of automatons patrolled. As her father had told her, each of these was a mostly lifelike replica of one of the former presidents of the United States. She could make out several versions of Abraham Lincoln, all wearing his signature stovepipe hat and keeping a close eye on the workers along the assembly line. Although Lincoln and the other former presidents looked to be life-sized, they carried the bulky rifles with ease.

Eleanor leaned slightly over the railing of the catwalk, trying to get a better look at the end of Ulysses S. Grant's cigar, which glowed orange, but emitted no smoke. One of the James Madison automatons swiveled his head completely around, and pointed in her direction. George Washington and Thomas Jefferson took aim with their rifles, and Eleanor tried to duck.

# TIMESLIP

Before she could move, however, a strong arm grabbed her from behind. She felt her feet lift off the catwalk just as a hail of bullets tore through the wooden beams. A moment later, Eleanor landed on another part of the catwalk, protected from the gunfire by a thick brick wall. The arm around her waist released as soon as she had her footing.

Eleanor spun around to face her assailant. The man behind her was dressed much like she was. He wore a long cloak with the hood pulled up, but obscured the top half of his face with a small domino mask in solid black. He held a single finger to his lips in warning, and then glanced at the bow.

"Huntsman?" he asked. "I didn't think you'd be up and about so quickly."

"I'm a quick healer. Why did you move me?" she whispered, trying to keep her voice both quiet and deeper than normal.

"You looked like you were about to get shot," the man suggested with a shrug. "You're lighter than I expected."

"I'm glad I am," Eleanor huffed. "You might have dropped me otherwise."

The man's eyes widened slightly, but he said nothing in response.

"This is hardly fair. You know who I am, and that I'd been injured, but I haven't a clue who you are. How do I know you're not working for whoever runs this place?"

"I, er... I'm a bit new to this scene." The faintest hint of a blush crept across his lower face. "In fact, this is the first time I've tried this whole defender of the people thing."

Eleanor tried to hide her smile. "What shall I call you?"

"How about Booth?" He suggested, a smile spreading across his face. "I was thinking it might be about time to pay our ex-presidents a quick visit from above. I wonder if I'd be hailed as a murderer or a savior in this case?"

"I wouldn't recommend it, either way. It'd be a nasty fall."

"Falling is for amateurs. I descend and ascend with perfect grace."

# TIMESLIP

Eleanor walked away without replying, rolling her eyes. She stepped to the edge of the brickwork, trying to see what had transpired below. Several of the automatons had clustered beneath the spot where they had shot out the catwalk, but they had not yet located the hiding pair. Production continued unabated, though another human had joined the workers. This one carried a sheaf of blueprints in one hand, while his other hand adjusted a monocle covering his right eye.

"That's Gregor Timonov," Eleanor muttered. "So that answers the question of who made the automatons."

"But why with the faces of ex-Presidents? And what's so interesting about those guns?"

"I haven't worked that part out yet. What do you do other than graceful falling?"

Booth reached for one edge of his cloak and drew it back, revealing row upon row of tiny snug pockets, each containing a shining vial filled with a liquid or powder. "Chemical compounds. I've got a little bit of everything here. What are you looking for?"

Eleanor smiled, reaching for one of her arrows. "How about a quick distraction while I snatch those plans?"

Booth selected two vials from his cloak and edged along the catwalk to a clear vantage point. Eleanor nocked an arrow attached to an almost imperceptibly thin length of cord. "Say the word," Booth whispered.

"On three," Eleanor replied, and then tapped her foot in three steady beats. She loosed the arrow as Booth hurled both of his vials toward the factory floor.

Their timing proved impeccable. Her arrow pierced the center of the plans just as a large cloud of white smoke blossomed up from Timonov's feet. As he and the other workers began coughing, Eleanor gave the cord a quick tug, and her arrow and the plans flew out of the smoke and directly into her hand.

She turned to Booth with a smile. "Now, to find someone to read these."

# TIMESLIP

Eleanor glanced around before she climbed down from her horse. The alleys of Cobalt City were dark, and she was certain that she had not been followed, but she knew to remain on the alert at all times.

Booth had remained at the warehouse, trying to learn more about the automatons, while Eleanor had taken the blueprints to an old family friend. She had implored Booth to not do anything rash in her absence, but the acrobatic chemist's eyes had gleamed when he promised to behave. She hoped she would not find him dead or the warehouse no longer standing.

As she rounded the corner, she exhaled gently. The warehouse was intact. But the rope that Booth had dropped out a window for her speedy exit was no longer hanging down the side of the building. Eleanor's eyes darted to the window where the rope should have been, and saw it neatly coiled on the ledge. She began to curse Booth under her breath, when a hint of movement at ground level caught her eye.

Two of the automatons, replicas of Andrew Jackson and Zachary Taylor, rounded the corner of the building. Their measured steps and swiveling heads reminded Eleanor of tin soldiers on parade. Both of the automatons rested large rifles against one shoulder, like sentries.

Rather than continuing around the perimeter of the building, however, the automatons stopped near the spot where she had landed. Jackson bent at the waist and studied the ground, while Taylor's head continued to rotate.

"Time to see what these things are really made of," she muttered as she aimed an arrow at Taylor's right eye. It hit solidly, creating a spray of sparks and stopping the construct dead in its tracks. Jackson did not look up, even when Taylor began emitting a high-pitched whine. A thin stream of steam erupted from the hole created by her arrow.

At the exact instant that Taylor's head exploded, Jackson moved. He flowed effortlessly to Taylor's side and seized the now nonfunctional automaton's weapon. Stabilizing himself on one knee, he hefted a rifle in each hand, and Eleanor found herself staring at the business ends of two of the oversized rifles.

She froze for only half a second, then dropped into a low crouch. The muzzles of the weapons followed her movement. "Old Hickory" pulled the triggers, but his weapons did not fire.

Taking advantage of the guns' malfunction, Eleanor sighted an arrow and aimed for Jackson's right eye. Without pausing to draw breath, she loosed the arrow. Jackson's fingers twitched on both triggers, but Eleanor had rolled out of the way before bullets began clattering out of the barrels.

"Ladies first, then," Eleanor murmured.

She waited long enough to see the second automaton's head combust, and then moved forward to examine the weapons. She did not attempt to lift either, but simply looked them over for the several joins that her father's friend had pointed out. At the base of each barrel, a narrow gap allowed the volatile bullets to "breathe." Satisfied, she closed the distance to the wall, where she found Booth watching out the window. He lowered the rope and Eleanor began to climb, soon aided by Booth pulling the rope hand over hand.

She climbed through the window unaided. "The weapons are modified Gatling guns. They probably weigh fifty or sixty pounds each, so that explains why the automatons are wielding them. The ammunition has magnesium in its core..."

"So it makes a bright light when it hits the air. Not quite sure about the practical application of that," Booth mused. Suddenly, he snapped his fingers. "Oh, but it will burn like the devil himself, especially if we can get it wet!"

"That's what my source believes as well. So Timonov has created his own personal army, more powerful than anyone else in the city. Luckily, the guns can be destroyed with an accurate shot, but I'm not sure about the automatons. Either way, once I hit one of either, it's likely to bring unwanted attention."

Booth rummaged through the tiny pockets lining his cloak. "Can you fire an accurate shot if there's a small vial attached to your arrow?"

"I believe so. What will the vial do?"

"Ignite the bullets, make the rifle explode. If we're lucky, trigger a few of the nearby rifles to do the same. Maybe take off a few of the automaton's heads in the process. That does seem to shut them down."

"Then you need to make sure that the workers have left the building before I start firing. Give me the vials and ten minutes to get them attached."

"Make it twenty if you want everyone human out. They change shifts at midnight. I should be able to have a few constables here by then. And you'll want to be ready to get out yourself, preferably unseen and unharmed." Booth's hand lingered on Eleanor's as he handed her the fragile vials. She tried to put his charming smile out of her mind as she began assembling her arrows.

Eleanor slid her finger across one of the modified arrows, testing its balance. Finally satisfied, she waited for the chiming of the St. Alban's bells. As soon as they began to toll the midnight hour, Eleanor readied her bow. Booth had been correct about the workers, as they all filed toward the entrance of the warehouse. She sighted along the arrow to locate the vulnerable point on one of the guns, and fired. Booth's vial shattered on impact, and the gun exploded in a burst of white light that quickly transformed into fierce flames. Eleanor found herself smiling at her effectiveness as three more guns suffered a similar fate, all from the flames of the first.

She reached for another arrow, but found that she could not draw the one she grasped from the quiver. She reached for another, but it was similarly stuck in place. In frustration, she tugged harder, mangling the feathers at the end. The arrow finally pulled free, but as she moved to nock the arrow, she realized that the vial she had so carefully tied to the arrow was missing. She slipped the quiver from her back and began looking at her arrows. The vial had been crushed by the pressure of pulling the arrow out, and the contents were rapidly saturating the nearby arrows with whatever chemical Booth had provided her. With a faint cry, she dumped the contents of the quiver onto the catwalk, and began salvaging the arrows that were still intact.

Below her on the warehouse floor, the automatons moved around and scanned the upper portions of the space. With only five arrows pulled from the wreckage of the quiver, the sounds of gunfire forced Eleanor to roll away from her position. The gunfire continued, filling the air with an almost sulfurous odor.

Eleanor yelped as her legs plunged into empty space. She reminded herself again that she needed to be fitted for men's pants, as her skirt caught on a splintered board, arresting her downward motion. She found herself flailing about as she tried to get a grasp on the nearby catwalk before additional bullets came her way.

Eleanor looked around, panic evident on her face. Booth slipped in through one of the upper windows and surveyed the situation. A flash of fear slipped across his normally jocular features, but he quickly mastered it. He tossed a hook and rope at one of the ceiling crossbeams, then swung across the open space to lift Eleanor out of her predicament.

As he set her down on solid catwalk for the second time tonight, he murmured into her ear. "Huntsman, I realize you're a well respected hero, but perhaps you should leave the lacy drawers at home when you're investigating crimes."

Eleanor gasped and looked down at her dress, which had fallen back into place over her underclothing. Her face felt hot as she arranged the cloak to cover the sizable rip in her riding clothing. She kept her face hidden, too embarrassed even to speak. Booth similarly remained silent.

After a long minute, Eleanor looked up to try to explain herself to Booth. Beyond his shoulder, she saw Timonov, flanked by two of his automatons. "Hide," she whispered. Booth ducked into the shadows, trying to pull her along with him.

Eleanor remained standing on the catwalk, the ruined portion between her and Timonov. She held her father's bow loosely in her left hand, and the remaining arrows in her right. As Timonov drew closer, he saw both. "Huntsman. I should have known that it was you who disrupted my patrolmen earlier. And now you've come back to seal your fate?"

Just off to her left, Booth whispered. "Keep your face covered. I'll do the talking." Then, a voice just as deep as Timonov's answered. "Timonov. Run now, while you have the chance." Eleanor darted a quick glance in Booth's direction and saw that he had found a long tube, through which he was speaking. The tube amplified and deepened his voice to a good approximation of Hiram Castille at his best.

"Why should I run when I have you cornered, Huntsman?"

Before Booth could speak again, Eleanor had raised the bow and all five arrows. "Because I'm faster than those hunks of metal," she snapped, the tautness of her voice echoing the twang of the bowstring.

Timonov's scream and two hissing sounds informed her of the accuracy of her shots. Looking up, she saw that the central arrow had pierced Timonov's monocle, while the two arrows to either side had scored direct hits on the heads of the automatons. As steam leaked from the automaton's heads, blood flowed from Timonov's eye.

Booth turned to look out the window, and used his makeshift speaking horn to call out to the constables below. With no arrows remaining, Eleanor faded back into the shadows with Booth to let the constabulary finish the job.

Eleanor slipped into the house through the servant's entrance, and was surprised to see her father sitting on a divan in the hallway. "Father, shouldn't you be in bed?"

"Shouldn't you still be on your way to Louis's estate?"

Eleanor hung her head. "I'm sorry. I went to the warehouse against your wishes. I just…"

"Constable Cooper stopped by on his way home to drop off the Huntsman's quiver, since I know our beloved hero. He said Huntsman did a 'bang up' job of catching Timonov." Hiram paused. "Thank you."

"What?" Eleanor looked up, stunned.

"Thank you for ensuring that the people of Cobalt City know that they can count on the Huntsman. I didn't want you to risk your life in my stead, but it seems that perhaps my fears were unfounded. You have the skills necessary to be the Huntsman, and you bore the mantle well."

Eleanor choked back a sob as she rushed to hug her father.

"Doctor Mathias says that I should rest for at least three weeks before I take up my nocturnal activities again. If you promise me that you will call for help whenever you need it, you may take on the role until I have healed."

"Oh, I promise! Thank you, Father! Thank you! I've even found someone who I can call on for help, and you will be able to call on him as well."

Hiram kissed Eleanor's cheek through the tears of joy. "Wonderful, you can tell me all about him later. Now, help me into that ridiculous wheelchair that the doctor left. It's not as though my legs are badly hurt. But he'll be very cross with me if his son reports back to him that I've been walking around."

"His son?"

"Yes. I'm not certain why, but he sent his son, Booth, over just a few minutes ago."

Eleanor gasped. "Doctor Mathias's son's name is Booth?"

"Yes," Hiram replied slowly. "Curious, Olivia said that he asked after you first, but I told her that I would see him. It's not proper for a young man to call on a young lady at this time of night, regardless of the errand. Do you know him?"

"I don't, but the Huntsman does," Eleanor answered with a twinkle in her eye.

*Dawn Vogel has edited non-fiction books about Abraham Lincoln and Ulysses S. Grant, but this is the first time the former presidents have found their way into her fiction writing. She works as a historical researcher, traveling and seeing the sights all over the country with her nose buried in dusty old records. In her alleged spare time, she runs a craft business, trains as a roller derby referee, and tries to work on a historical fantasy young adult novel.*
*Dawn lives in Seattle with her awesome boyfriend Jeremy and their herd of cats. She can be found online at* http://scarywhitegirl.net.

# TIMESLIP

## Claws of the Dragon Queen
## A Wrecker of Engines Story
## 1949

Bang! Bang!

The watcher on the opposite roof leaped up and raced toward the fire escape.

Two shots, barely a heartbeat between them, two flashes of light in the darkened apartment across the street. Sammy Mongo must be home. And somebody else already had intercepted him.

The Wrecker of Engines cursed softly behind his porcelain mask as he lunged down the fire escape, not bothering with the final ladder. He leapt out from the landing, his Oriental training dropping him cat-soft upon the sidewalk below.

This night, his careful detective work looked to end in murder. He knew the sounds of those shots: two Colt 45s, the guns favored by Sammy Mongo.

Fast-draw Sammy would have hit whoever was hidden in his apartment and then be out the door, taking such secrets with him as the current whereabouts of Dr. Caesar.

The Wrecker of Engines raced to the back of building, guessing Sammy would take the alley exit. He still had time could to catch the gangster before Sammy disappeared into Cobalt City's darker neighborhoods. But the alley was empty. For once, he was wrong. The crook must have gone out the front.

He put his hand on the back door of the little apartment building. Already, in the apartments above, he could hear lights being switched on, anxious questions shouted. Two shots, well after midnight, even in this part of town, somebody would be dialing the operator and asking for the police.

No time for hesitation. Once the flatfoots arrived, no hope to find any evidence of where the elusive Sammy had fled. He took the stairs two at a time, cracking the door open on the landing of the third floor, the floor where Sammy lived.

No one moved in the dimly lit hallway. The neighbors might be calling the cops but nobody was coming to investigate on their own.

The Wrecker of Engines slipped down the hall to Sammy's door. Unlocked and slightly open. The apartment beyond was dark.

Pulling a maroon-and-ivory flip light out of his pocket, the Wrecker of Engines cautiously rolled the flashlight's beam around the room. A pair of polished men's shoes, black silk socks encasing the heavy ankles, good wool trousers. The Wrecker played the beam up the man's body even as he crossed the room for closer look.

It was Sammy Mongo. And, given that his body was the only one cooling rapidly on the apartment's cheap rag rug, for once Sammy Mongo had missed his target.

Two Colts lay on the floor, just inches from his outstretched hands. A quick sniff of the barrels confirmed that both guns had been shot just minutes before.

The Wrecker did a fast visual search of the room, moving the flashlight with a steady hand to illuminate each corner and then pass beyond. The place was as tidy as might be expected for a bachelor gangster with no steady doll to keep him in order.

Two bullets had punched holes in the plaster of the wall opposite of where Sammy lay. No blood splatters. He had definitely missed his target; surprising for a man feared throughout the tongs for his deadly accuracy.

The Wrecker of Engines turned the light back on the corpse for one last look. Already he could hear sirens wailing up the street. The cops were on their way.

Sammy was sprawled flat, face down. No visible wound. He rolled him over. The suit was clean, no bullet holes from head to heel. Well, he hadn't heard a third shot, so that made sense, although he could see no sign of what had actually killed the killer.

Then the Wrecker of Engines noticed that one of Sammy's hands was clenched in a fist. He pried the dead man's fingers open. A white jade hairpin carved in the shape of a clawing dragon dropped onto the carpet. This was no bauble from Woolworths—such ornaments once decorated the heads of Chinese noblewomen.

# TIMESLIP

He heard voices, the elevator cage creaking up the front of the building. The police had arrived and it was time for him to go.

The Wrecker of Engines hesitated for moment. He disliked making the job more difficult for the boys in blue who fought crime in Cobalt City. But his instincts kept him alive and the scourge of evil scientists. He swooped down and grabbed the hairpin, pocketing that one piece of evidence before slipping noiselessly out of the apartment and down the backstairs.

On the street, he pulled the porcelain mask off, rotating it in his hand to stare into at the hexagram painted across its smooth surface. Shih Ho: the hexagram 21 of the I Ching, his reminder to all that without justice, balance was unattainable. He slipped the mask inside his suit jacket and shoved his black fedora higher his forehead. He buttoned up his trench coat to hide his own handguns. Satisfied that his Webleys were well concealed, he ambled to the front door.

The cop standing next to car was a guy he knew.

"Hey, Johnny," he said as he pulled a pocket notebook and pencil from his coat pocket, "what's with the midnight house call?"

"Wilde," replied the young patrolman with a start. "Where did you come from?"

"Ah, you know how it is, slow news night, thought I might as well take a walk around, see if there is any action."

Johnny Maguire shook his honest, red head. "You reporters, you must have a sixth sense or something. There was a murder up there, less than a half hour ago. Detectives just went up to take a look."

"Heard who the body is?" Wilde asked.

"Some Chinese gangster. Guy named Sammy Mongo. Chief's been after him for years for people smuggling, but he's slick. Every time that we'd get close, he'd disappear, wait for the heat to die down, then come back to Cobalt City."

The coroner's truck pulled up behind Johnny's patrol car.

"Looks like he's going on his last trip now," said Wilde.

"Sure does," replied Johnny. "I wonder who got him."

"So do I, so do I," murmured Wilde, dropping one hand into his pocket and tracing the white jade dragon hairpin with his fingertips.

# TIMESLIP

Once the club had been a celebrated hotspot, infamous in the 1920s for the mysterious disappearance of a jazz pianist. Twenty years later, the place was just another dive, full of sailors, dollar-a-dance girls, and other flotsam of Cobalt City's docks. But a hot tip from a cool dame at the teashop down the block led Wilde to his current seat at the bar. According to Lady Pekoe, Sammy Mongo came here regularly, working with the tongs to provide safe passage for certain criminals looking to leave Cobalt City for less hero-ridden climes.

Wilde suspected that Mongo's latest client was Dr. Caesar. The nasty Italian had struck a deal with the OSS to skip his master Mussolini's fate by bringing his Project Pompeii to the Allies. But for months, Wilde had been hearing rumors that Dr. Caesar was trying to peddle his lava bomb elsewhere. He'd slipped the OSS boys back in London, hopped the Atlantic, and then scampered to Cobalt City faster than a man could say "Spaghetti Bolognese."

The less-than-good doctor did an excellent job of hiding. None of Wilde's usual sources could turn up a lead. A solid month of hunting only yielded one clue. A frightened little man in a shiny suit whispered "Marco Polo" at an exhibition of Italian Renaissance paintings.

If his source was right, Dr. Caesar meant to follow another famous Italian to fame and fortune in the Far East. It fit the man's pattern—basing his crimes on the exploits of Italian heroes—previously he'd tried to take over the world from Alexandria before being sunk at Actium. Lucky for the Allies that the Queen of the Nile refused to play Cleopatra to his Mark Antony. The Egyptian super-heroine used her asps to good effect then.

Wilde slid a quarter from finger to finger, making it disappear and reappear. Anyone looking at the bar would see just a tired hack, grabbing a highball before heading back to the night desk. The roving reporter disguise let him wander where he wanted, even into the laboratories of industrials, government geniuses, and mad scientists, not that he ever saw a difference. It was all matters of degree and every degree dealt death to the innocent, as far as he was concerned. Let them build their engines of destruction: he would find them and destroy them.

But first he had to unearth Dr. Caesar from his current hidey-hole. With luck, the lunatic Latin hadn't heard about Sammy's sudden demise and would still come here to arrange his passage to the Orient.

He flipped the quarter one last time, making it vanish in midair.

"You make magic. I make magic too," a Chinese woman slid onto the barstool next to him. She wore a crimson cheongsam dress, the embroidered silk caressing every curve like a lover, from the high collar to the long slit up her left thigh. Her dark hair was piled high and secured with a green jade ornament carved in the shape of a dragon. With a quick glance, he knew immediately that she was no working girl.

The lady pulled a cigarette from the tiny black satin handbag dangling from one wrist.

With a practiced flip of the fingers, Wilde made a lit match appear and held it to the tip.

She drew in her breath and then blew it out, pursing the scarlet-painted lips to create one perfect smoke ring to float as fragile as a soap bubble before them.

"Magic," she whispered.

He laughed. He rarely did, not like that, a true rolling laugh that made heads turn in the bar, seeking the sound of a man's delight.

"The name's Wilde," he said.

She smiled but said nothing more.

"Can I buy you a drink?"

She shook her head and gave a tiny shrug, barely a ripple of silk. Her eyes never left the room, her glance lightly grazing and then discarding every man.

"Can I help you find someone?" A true shot in the smoky dark, but there was something about the way that she sat, so still, so calm, and so very conscious of everyone around them. He knew that pose, knew it like he knew his own skin, for once he'd trained with the masters who taught that perfect stillness of utter awareness. The tranquility of the tiger, one old woman called it, long ago in a temple at the top of wind-wracked mountain.

She shook her head, a regretful moue of those faultless lips.

In the back of the club, somebody plunked a nickel into the jukebox and punched the latest romantic hit by Perry Como. The dollar-a-dance girls shrugged themselves off the wall and began to circulate the room, sliding with tired sensuality around the tables to trail their fingertips along one masculine shoulder or another.

At the doorway, a group of men entered, chatting among themselves, pulling off hats and scarves, waving at the cigarette girl to come closer.

Beside him, the mysterious beauty in red focused suddenly on one man hanging slightly behind the others. It was just the slightest twitch, a heel planted more firmly on the floor, the fingers loosening just slightly on the cigarette, ready to discard it.

He looked beyond her, letting his senses open, seeing exactly what she saw. The man by the door, the hat pulled low and the white velvet muffler swathed around his chin to disguise a distinctive jaw line. But nothing could hide that grand Roman nose.

"Dr. Caesar!" He barely breathed the name as he left from his barstool. But as quickly as he moved, the scarlet cheongsam was first to reach Mussolini's favorite scientist. Her long fingers reached up, and a blur of red nails raked Dr. Caesar's cheek. The irritated Italian whirled away, staggered, and fell in a crumpled heap across the entrance.

Wilde barely paused to check for a pulse. Even as his fingers touched the corpse, he knew that Dr. Caesar would never reach the Far East.

On the jukebox, Como crooned about an enchanted evening. But Wilde saw that his beautiful stranger already had left the room. He followed her into the night, leaving behind the gathering storm of exclamations as the others in the club realized a dead man blocked the doorway.

The mask was cool against his face as he trailed the slender shadow down the alley. Somewhere a cat hissed in warning as one of

# TIMESLIP

Cobalt City's mutant rats scampered over the garbage cans and up a wall. From the open window high above, the crackle of the radio nearly drowned out the fight between the thin woman and her fat husband over his disappearing paycheck.

All these sounds registered and were ignored. "Be always aware, never overwhelmed, concentrate on the one shadow among the many," the old mask maker had said as he poured a thin stream of steaming green tea into the translucent porcelain cups. It was a lesson that he never forgot.

The Wrecker of Engines continued down the alley, past the rundown apartment buildings, letting the noises of the night fall behind him as he followed the mysterious woman in scarlet.

Now his particular shadow slipped into a doorway. The flickering light bulb barely illuminated her lovely face as she knocked twice, paused, and then knocked twice once more.

An eyehole in the door slid open. A muted exchange ensued. Too far away to make out the actual words, the Wrecker of Engines still recognized the fluting cadences as Mandarin, the preferred dialect of Northern China.

The door opened and she hurried inside. As she passed directly under the light, he caught another glimpse of the intricate jade hair ornament securing her chignon.

He waited for a few minutes. Then he scanned the side of the building. Against all city regulations, there was no fire escape to allow easy egress or entry to the upper floors. More telling, all the windows to the roof were barred. The steel bars looked suspiciously new and secure. The large moon overhead revealed a telltale glitter along the roofline: broken glass to cut any rope thrown up there with a grappling hook. Whoever defended this building knew the peculiar talents of Cobalt City's villains and heroes.

Now which, he wondered, as he made his own quiet exit from the alley, did they fear?

A quick reconnaissance at the front of the building showed an equal amount of fortification. The ground floor business was an

88

importer of Oriental antiquities, with heavy lacquered red-and-gold doors ornamentally bolted and barred against night intruders.

Disguised under the curlicues of black iron, the Wrecker of Engines spotted a Springhold triple-action lock, the type favored by banks and government offices, nearly impossible to pick without the right tools. He fingered the black leather case in his trench coat pocket. He had the right tools, of course, but the streetlamps in this section seemed unnaturally bright. Directly across the street from his intended target was an all-night diner with large plate glass windows. Even from his shadowed corner at the mouth of the alley, he could easily pick out the white-jacketed counterman and his late night customers slumped over their coffee cups.

Any man attempting the front of the building would be spotted immediately. It would be easier and less conspicuous to come back during daylight hours.

Slipping off the mask, Wilde turned on his heel, intent on some research. The green jade hairpin that she wore so carefully inserted into her ebony braids—he was certain that the design was the same as the white jade hairpin found clutched in Sammy Mongo's dead hand.

When his own library proved unusually inadequate, Wilde sought out the only man in Cobalt City with an even greater collection of Oriental history.

Professor Norman Chandler returned from the mysterious East with an ailment that left his body crippled but his mind intact. Through a large endowment, paid in gold coins according to certain gossips, he persuaded the Adventurer's Club to let him turn the top floor of their brownstone building into his own private residence. He had his meals sent up from the Club's kitchens, had his rooms cleaned and his errands run by the Club's staff, and his visitors vetted and announced by the Club's doorman.

With a nod at the doorman, Wilde went straight to the Professor's private elevator. A push of the button and it whisked him to the entry hall of Chandler's apartment.

"In the library," called out the Professor as Wilde paused to hang his hat and coat on the oak hallstand.

There, Wilde found Chandler settled in his favorite leather chair, a cigar and a brandy on the little brass table at his elbow, and a pulp magazine resting in his lap. His ivory canes were propped neatly against the wall, within easy reach if needed.

"You'll forgive me if I don't rise?" the Professor gave his usual greeting. "Help yourself to a drink, you know where."

Wilde smiled and strode to the sidebar, with its ornate cut glass decanters all clearly labeled in sterling silver. Ice from the leather bucket, a splash of soda water, and a healthy shot of the Professor's excellent Scotch were quickly mixed. He pulled up a chair next to the Professor.

"Cigarette?" said his host, indicating the cloisonné box on his table.

Wilde shook his head. "I never smoke."

"Really?" said Chandler. "I thought all you detective types smoked hard, drank harder, and chased anything wearing a skirt."

Wilde chuckled. "You should never believe what you read in those magazines."

"Oh, this?" said the Professor. He held up the magazine so Wilde could see the cover. An Asian giant with brilliant green skin and a queue that reached down to his bare back straddled a shrieking blonde while a man with two smoking guns lunged through a door at the pair. "I read these as part of my research into the current Western attitude toward the other half of the world. Fascinating bits of truth mangled by the jaws of the commercial hyenas who publish this debased entertainment for the masses."

"I thought you had a story in this issue."

"I do," said Chandler. "But they gave the cover to some Dutchman writing about an Asian mastermind with fiendish minions. And buried my serial of lost civilizations high in the Himalayas in the back. According to the bloodsucking sensationalist who I laughingly call an editor, shrieking blondes in red lace tops and torn skirts sell better than sturdy explorers in khaki."

"So add a blonde to your next chapter," suggested Wilde.

"And defile the purity of my tale!" Chandler snorted. "I'm outraged!" He sipped his brandy and took a couple of puffs on his cigar before replacing it in the bronze holder shaped like a miniature sacrificial cauldron of the late Han dynasty. "Of course, she could be an immortal Viking princess, imprisoned in the temple."

"Wasn't there a Sultana infatuated with your explorer earlier?"

Chandler beamed at him. "You do read my work! But she died on the sacrificial alter, taking a knife to the heart intended for my hero. That month I did get the cover." Chandler took another sip of brandy. "A Viking princess, her fur robes slipping down to reveal the white purity of....hmmm....yes, I can see that appealing to the hyena. Very good, Wilde, very good. Now that we've solved my little literary problem, what can I do for you?"

Wilde pulled the white jade hairpin from his breast pocket and handed it to Chandler. At once his chuckling host became the serious scholar, dropping the magazine into a basket by his chair and pulling out a small magnifying glass from his pocket.

"Quite fine," he said. "No flaws or discoloration in the jade. Exquisite detail. And a ruby...no...a pink diamond, quite rare, for the eye. It's an imperial dragon, of course."

"Yes," said Wilde. "Five claws."

"But a woman's hair ornament." Chandler tapped his magnifying glass against his lower lip. "Where have I seen this beauty before?"

"I could find no reference in my collection."

"Most likely not. If this is what I think it is. Third shelf from the top, the fourth volume from the left."

Wilde went to the bookcase that the Professor indicated. He pulled the slim blue book from the shelf and handed it to his friend.

Chandler flicked through the pages. "Ah, there you are." He flipped the book around so Wilde could see the sketch of five hairpins, each one exactly like the one now resting on the Professor's gray, flannel-covered knee.

"So what are they?"

"Loosely translated, the Dragon Queen's Claws. Five hairpins, each made from a different shade of jade, each containing a deadly secret." Chandler set down the book and his magnifying glass to pick up the white jade hairpin. His thin, clever fingers ran the length of the long jade spike that formed the dragon's tail and up again to the head. "Ah, here, the eye, of course." He pressed the pink diamond eye of the dragon and a steel needle sprang out of the dragon's tail. He tested it lightly with one fingertip, drawing a droplet of blood. "Razor sharp. Driven with the proper force and placement into the base of the skull..."

"It could kill a man instantly," Wilde nodded. "But this one was found in a dead man's fist."

"Then it isn't what killed him," said Chandler. "But, remember, there is more than one claw. According to reports filed by one rather questionable eyewitness during the Opium Wars, the man who made those sketches, the five hairpins were doled out by the Empress to her favorite assassins. All ladies, by the way, and all trained to kill with a variety of innocent objects that might be found in any lady's possession: a silk scarf, an ivory chopstick, a paper fan, or a jade hairpin."

"The scratch of a painted fingernail?"

"Certainly. I've seen that done with certain poisons in Singapore."

Wilde grunted, sipping the remains of his Scotch. "But there is no Empress of China. The entire royal family either fled to the West or was captured by the Japanese. They say the last Emperor is a gardener now, quite happy to trim the shrubs and spout Communist maxims after being rescued by the Chairman's army."

"Poor old chap, he was never all that keen to be Emperor in the first place. I met him once, a little boy bicycling about the Forbidden City. But there were rumors at the end of the war, odd things stirring out in the hinterlands. Have you ever heard of a city called Xian?"

"The tomb of the First Emperor?"

The Professor nodded. "So legend says. A large grassy knoll. The locals grazed their animals across it when I was there. Supposedly an entire city is buried beneath it."

"With rivers of mercury and palaces of silver and jade. And an entire army of living clay soldiers to defend it."

Chandler nodded. "Quite the fairy tale. But, after the war, a number of imperial treasures were discovered to be missing from the Forbidden City. The Communists blamed the Japanese, the Japanese blamed the General, and the General issued edicts from his island that he has nothing. The most notable loss was the jewels of the Empress, a collection that included this white jade hairpin."

"And what does this have to do with Xian?"

"The Communists have closed all roads going there. All trains. All air transport. There was talk of a natural disaster, an earthquake or a flood, devastating the region. And, of course, with China's borders sealed tight, reports these days are sketchy and unreliable."

"But?"

"There's an interesting rumor swirling around certain circles. That a new Forbidden City has risen out of the tomb of the First Emperor. An imperial city ruled by a Dragon Queen."

"With her own cadre of female assassins?"

"Quite possibly." The Professor rolled the hairpin in his fingers, making the pink diamond eye glitter. "There have been some unexplained murders. Hong Kong, Singapore, Bombay, San Francisco. All scientists or businessmen. All rumored to be supporters of the Communists and, thus, not necessarily our best friends. Quite possibly someone from our side is responsible."

Wilde raised one eyebrow in question. He had never seen the Professor look so troubled.

"However," said Chandler, placing the white jade hairpin carefully on the table between them, "based on the inquiries that I've received from certain people that I cannot name, I suspect our covert friends are just as baffled as the police. But one common tale is told for all: each victim was seen with an Oriental woman of surpassing beauty shortly before dying."

"Would an Italian scientist with a fondness for volcanic explosions be a typical victim?"

"Not an unreasonable guess."

"I cannot say that I will mourn the man," said Wilde slowly, revolving his drink in his hand, making the ice tinkle like a wind chime. "But I dislike murder in my city, no matter how noble the cause. If these ladies of death are here, I will find them."

"Do you need a bed for tonight?"

Wilde shook his head. "I do not intend to sleep until this is solved. If I grow tired, a few minutes meditation in a quiet corner will be sufficient. I find the public library very restorative."

Chandler chuckled. "Nice line. I may use it in my next thriller."

"I'm sure your own adventures are more than adequate fodder for the pulps. My life," Wilde said, "is not nearly sensational enough for your editor."

"Hmm," said the Professor, "I do wonder if you ever tell me the entire truth of your investigations."

"More than any other man, Chandler, more than any other. I appreciate your help tonight."

"And this deadly little memento?" Chandler held up the hairpin.

"Keep it safe," said Wilde as he strode out the door.

He waited until late afternoon, that hour when clerks tend to drowse and even the finest of secretaries ease their toes from their high-heeled shoes and dream about a second cup of coffee. Or, in the case of the sole lady working in the office of an Oriental importer of antiquities, a nicely brewed cup of tea.

Miss Hong, a secretary with the steel-framed glasses and hair clipped too short for any type of ornament, looked longingly at her fragrantly steaming pot and waiting cup. Then she audibly stifled a sigh before turning back to Wilde.

"So you need to tour our entire warehouse? Could you not just give me a list of the items needed, sir?"

"Oh, no, no!" Wilde waved his hands fluidly through the air, finishing with an emphatic flutter of the fingertips. "I am creating a palace, a true palace, of absolutely decadent Asian splendor... although, between you and me, nobody is going to notice my creative talents with the seventeen *houris* in peacock feathers rushing around, trying to distract the prince from saving his red-haired princess."

"I'm sorry," said Miss Hong, blinking her eyes rapidly at this speech. "I do not understand, Mister?"

"Hawthorne, Septimus Hawthorne, set designer for Lew Large Productions." With his conjurer's fingers, he produced the white-and-gold business card that he used for this persona. "We're creating a new spectacle in Technicolor based on Aladdin. And when Lew's clever little scriptwriter discovered that Aladdin is from China, not Persia, so Lew said to me: no scimitars and brass, no tacky flying carpets. Make it look like old China. The real thing. Emperor's palace."

Miss Hong sighed and reached into her desk to gather up the keys to the company's backrooms. She slid her feet slowly back into her shoes.

"Oh, dearie," fluted Wilde, "it can take me hours, simply hours, to find the right little knickknacks for Lew. Why don't you give Septimus those keys and you enjoy your little cup of tea."

"I don't know if that would be allowed...."

"I'll be extra, extra careful, darling, I promise. And if I so much as crack a vase, Lew will pay for the lot." He tilted his head and flung his hands up to his shoulders in an exaggerated shrug that he copied from one of Cobalt City's most infamous art thieves, the Yellow Daffodil. "That's the delightful thing about working for a mogul: he never cares how much one spends on his little endeavors."

With a more refined shrug of her own, Miss Hong handed over the keys and eagerly turned back to her teacup.

Past the inner doorway and out of sight, Wilde undid the buttons of his trench coat to allow free access to the deadly Webleys stored in the twin shoulder harnesses. He turned the pale purple ascot around his throat, an essential part of Septimus Hawthorne's character, inside out. Backed with black silk and lined with leather, the ascot became a collar to protect his throat from the garrote wire or the assassin's blade.

He pulled the porcelain mask from his pocket and settled on his face. He was no longer Wilde the amiable night reporter or Hawthorne the flamboyant Hollywood designer or the half dozen other characters he put on and off like Carnival masks. Now he was the Wrecker of Engines, the true man protected behind the gleaming black-and-white mask.

He made for the back of the building, stepping lightly through the cluttered bric-a-brac piled to the ceiling. Cloisonné vases large enough to hide a child, opium beds carved from rosewood, chests inlaid with mother-of-pearl decorations, fake antiques created for the export trade and meant to hide the true use of the building. For his sharp eyes spotted footsteps in the dust of the far corner, a man's heel half visible at the edge of a seemingly solid wall.

The Wrecker of Engines ran his fingers along the wooden boards of the warehouse wall, starting at the floor and working slowly upward. A few seconds of search, based on the position of the half visible footprint, and he found the catch that unlocked the secret door. Behind it was a staircase lit by bare bulbs leading upward.

He pulled the Webleys from their holsters, unwilling to climb weaponless that obvious an entrance to a villain's lair.

Someone had pounded the boards down tight on this stair, not a single tread creaked as he climbed. It seemed that the others using this particular route wanted to hide the sound of their passage. The straight staircase ended at plain wooden door, no keyhole, just a simple latch. He paused on the landing, pressing one ear against the panel of the door. Beyond it, he heard the musical rise and fall of Mandarin.

The Wrecker of Engines drew back a little and applied shoe leather to the door, kicking it wide open and leaping inside before the occupants had time to arm themselves.

Five women whipped around at his entrance. In the center was his scarlet-clad beauty. The four clustered around her were beauties as well, dressed in the colors of the peony, the orchard, the chrysanthemum, and the plum blossom. Each, except the woman in palest pink, wore a jade hairpin in the form of a rearing five-toed dragon, an imperial dragon of death.

Behind the mask, his laugh rang like mournful bell.

Strong men, murderers, had trembled when that laugh filled the room, exposing the rotted core of their souls. Scientists had clutched tubes of bubbling destruction and drank their own poison rather than face his knowing mockery.

But the servants of the Dragon Queen were different. They drew a little apart. One unlaced a silk scarf from around her throat, another unfurled a paper fan, the third casually lifted a chopstick from the table, and the fourth reached up to her braids to pluck out her jade hairpin.

"The laughter of the Lonely Man cannot frighten us," said the beauty in the center, the killer of Dr. Caesar. "We too have walked the path of fire through the iron temple."

"Then you know that to corrupt the arts of the incorruptible way leads to madness," said the Wrecker of Engines, his voice deep as the ocean and more fearsome than a storm at sea. "And the punishment of the just."

Two of the women faltered as he used the Voice of Doom upon them. But the woman in golden silk threw her paper fan at him, whirling it through the air. He heard the slicing sound of its hidden blades and leaped to one side. The very tip of the fan caught the shoulder of his trench coat and ripped it open.

He raised the Webleys, always his last resort, and fired twice: bang! bang! Just as Sammy Mongo had before these deadly lovelies murdered him.

The first shot shattered the chopstick in the hands of the woman in pink. The second ripped the silk scarf out of the grasp of the pretty killer in pale purple. He wouldn't kill a woman, not unless they forced him to it.

With silent speed, the lady in pure white silk sprang at him, her black jade hairpin unsheathed to reveal the deadly steel tip. He leaped to the side, only to find the crimson claws of the fifth assassin slashing at the edge of the mask. With a twist of his head, he avoided her. Her nails scratched uselessly against the smooth porcelain protecting his cheek.

# TIMESLIP

He rolled around her, reversing the gun in his hand to strike with the butt at the murderous white butterfly attempting to skewer him with her steel stiletto.

The woman gave a musical gasp and folded to the floor. Another of her sisters dashed forward to pull her from the fray.

The Wrecker of Engines flipped the gun again, lifting both Webleys now for a clear shot at his attackers. His back to the door, they could only come at him straight on.

"I can take you all with two shots," he proclaimed. The reverberation of this proclamation conferred by the tricks of the porcelain mask made them hesitate.

The scarlet-clad leader held up one hand. The others froze in place.

"Our business is done in Cobalt City," she said. "The madman is dead and our people are safe. I do not think that many others will hurry to sell their services to the Chairman, not when they know the toll that we demand."

"There are other ways than murder," he responded, the Webleys still and steady in his hands, one trained upon her heart.

"Blow up their laboratories by switching the labels on the chemicals that they mixed in their beakers? Unscrew the wires so their own bombs consumed them in flames? Pour sugar into the engines of airships so they crashed into the fields rather than rain bombs upon the innocent?"

"There were always warnings," he said. "Shih Ho. If they turned aside, if they followed the just way, if they did not use their terrible engines of destruction, they would not have reaped that whirlwind."

"But did your tricks save Hiroshima? Did your methods shelter Nagasaki?"

He gasped. Beneath the hexagram, the tears ran swiftly, silently, down his cheeks. His greatest shame, his greatest failure, his soul slashed into ribbons of remorse by her gentle voice.

"I knew you when I first saw you," she whispered so low that it seemed only he and she were in the room. "The warrior with the heart of heavenly fire."

And then, to the startled cries of the others, she extended one hand. "Come with us. Help us. Together we save China from a terrible war."

He hesitated, nearly seduced by her simple request. The Webleys dipped the barest fraction in his hands.

The blow came from one side, the forgotten dame in pink. She swung a clay camel with deadly accuracy, striking the base of his skull. He pitched forward, falling, falling into a cloud of crimson silk.

Two days later, Chandler watched him pour a scotch from the cut-glass decanter.

"Should you?" asked the Professor. "After all, that concussion left you unconscious for hours."

"I hurt my pride more than my head," replied Wilde. "An imitation Tang dynasty camel, of all things. And then to be discovered by Miss Hong in the warehouse."

"Decent of the Dragon Queen's ladies to remove your mask and hide your guns before leaving you on the warehouse floor."

"More decent to leave my mask for me in that hidden room. And the Webleys. I would have missed those. I've had them since my OSS days."

"So that's it," said Chandler. "Beaten by five ladies of more than Oriental splendor. I'm sure my editor would never accept that one."

Wilde shrugged. "We all have our defeats. As such things go, this one, I can live with." And still he could hear her whisper, 'Did your tricks save Hiroshima? Did your methods shelter Nagasaki?'

He rambled around the Professor's library, a restless striding to and fro. On the bookshelf, propped in front of a slim blue book, was the white jade hairpin.

Taking it from its place, Wilde rolled the hairpin between his fingers, making it appear and disappear. "Magic," he whispered.

The Professor watched with the eyes of a man who has seen his own dreams of adventure shatter with his health long ago.

"So, at least, you have a small souvenir," Chandler observed.

"Pity," said Wilde, "to break up a set like that." And, then, very abruptly, he added, "She left me a note. Draped around the mask."

"You hadn't mentioned that before."

Wilde pulled the rectangle of silk out of his pocket. He dropped it on the Professor's lap.

The scholar unrolled the former white scarf, the center showing a neat bullet hole. Chinese characters, painted in crimson ink, swirled like dancers down the silk.

"Come to me," Chandler translated.

Wilde nodded.

"Will you go?" the Professor asked.

He shrugged and the paper of the airplane ticket hidden in his breast pocket crackled like the first flame in a conflagration.

"The borders are closed," Wilde said. "Nobody goes in, nobody gets out. A foreigner, a white devil foreigner, would be spotted in a minute."

"Unless he hid his face behind a mask," Chandler said.

Wilde laughed, and it was the carefree laugh of the man and not the hollow laughter of the mask. He tossed the white jade hairpin into the air. He watched it twist, end over end, claws over tail, the pink diamond eye glittering in the lamplight. Then he snapped one hand out. The dragon vanished into his pocket.

"I'll send you a postcard," he promised his friend.

*Rosemary Jones has written two novels set in the Forgotten Realms:* Crypt of the Moaning Diamond *and* City of the Dead *(the latter now available as an e-book too!). She previously made a foray into Cobalt City for Christmas dinner. Her short stories appear in* Close Encounters of Urban Kind *(Apex),* Realms of the Dead *(WOTC),* Zero Gravity *(Pill Hill), and others. Unlike Professor Chandler, Rosemary has found her editors to be most understanding when it comes to deadlines and adventures set in the odder corners of the imagination. You can follow her fictional journeys at* www.rosemaryjones.com

# TIMESLIP

# TIMESLIP

## Afterword:
## A Note From the Creator

There are so many stories to tell in the Cobalt City universe. Thus far, I've written several short stories and four and one-half novels. I could write about nothing else and still never tap the full potential. Thankfully, other authors have been inspired by Cobalt City as much as I have. That *was* always the point.

Cobalt City was born a shared sandbox. Friends and family created the bulk of the Protectorate characters. The stories shared together were never written down – the magic of temporary art and shared creativity. The sandbox of Cobalt City quietly remained when those events ended. But the characters refused to remain silent. That's why I started the Cobalt City anthologies in 2009, with *Cobalt City Christmas.*

Looking for more excitement? Keep updated on future releases by visiting timidpirate.com, where you can submit your Cobalt City story starting June, 2011. Or save your pennies for the release of the anthology in Fall, 2011.

*Nathan Crowder*

www.ingramcontent.com/pod-product-compliance
Lightning Source LLC
Chambersburg PA
CBHW021122130626
46554CB00002B/819